Kill Him Twice
Richard S. Prather

AN [*e-reads*] BOOK
New York, NY

No part of this publication may be reproduced or transmitted in any form or by any means, electronic, or mechanical, including photocopy, recording, scanning or any information storage retrieval system, without explicit permission in writing from the Author.

This book is a work of fiction. Names, characters, places and incidents are products of the author's imagination or are used fictitiously. Any resemblance to actual events or locals or persons, living or dead, is entirely coincidental.

Copyright © 1965 by Richard S. Prather
First e-reads publication 2002
www.e-reads.com
ISBN 0-7592-2706-3

Other books by Richard S. Prather also available in e-reads editions

CASE OF THE VANISHING BEAUTY
BODIES IN BEDLAM
EVERYBODY HAD A GUN
FIND THIS WOMAN
THE SCRAMBLED YEGGS
WAY OF A WANTON
DAGGER OF FLESH
DARLING, IT'S DEATH
TOO MANY CROOKS
ALWAYS LEAVE 'EM DYING
PATTERN FOR PANIC
STRIP FOR MURDER
THE WAILING FRAIL
HAVE GAT-WILL TRAVEL
SLAB HAPPY
THREE'S A SHROUD
TAKE A MURDER, DARLING
OVER HER DEAR BODY
DOUBLE IN TROUBLE
DANCE WITH THE DEAD
DIG THAT CRAZY GRAVE
KILL THE CLOWN
JOKER IN THE DECK
THE COCKEYED CORPSE
DEAD HEAT
THE TROJAN HEARSE
DEAD MAN'S WALK

One

She raced past the carnivorous seaweed, leaped over a clump of man-eating yummym, and skirted the boiling-lava beds. She was wearing what appeared to be a negligee the color and thickness of thin fog, which slid up her thighs as she ran, bare legs flashing white in the sunlight. She was moving very speedily, but the giant oysters were still gaining on her. Clack-clack, went the oysters.

Her name was Cherry Dayne, spelled hoo-boy, and she was the kind of gal the people in my dreams dream about — five feet, five inches tall, a hundred and twenty pounds arranged 36-22-36 above those fabulous legs, and a face flaunting incandescent lips and acetylene-blue eyes, topped by beige-blonde hair the approximate shade of boiling honey. Yeah, it sure looked as if those oysters were going to get her. She'd run past the boiling-lava beds and stopped at the cliff's edge. Below the cliff was the horrible Lake of Fire. She was trapped.

Cherry screamed — very prettily.

And upon her the monster oysters advanced, clacking wildly.

Cherry screamed again, half an octave higher.

Clack-clack. "Eeeee." *Clack-Clack.* "*Eeeeeeee.*" CLACK-CLACK-CLACK! "EEEAAAAHHH!" "Cut!"

That "Cut!" was from director Walter Phrye, and just in time, too. In another second lovely Cherry Dayne would have been gobbled up and digested.

Phrye, for those not in the know — or not subscribers to *Inside* — is the genius who directed *The Day the Earth Cracked*, not to mention *Space Glop*, not to mention which is a pretty good idea, both of which had apparently been based on returned comic books. And this was, as you may have guessed, the location where Jeremy Slade's latest "monster movie" was being filmed.

You know monster movies — *The Day the Worms Turned*, *The Horrible Living Urp*, and so on. Well, this was Slade's latest, biggest, goofiest epic, *Return of the Ghost of the Creeping Goo*.

Study that title, will you? If examined with a rapier-like intelligence it will tell you a lot. It will tell you too much. Yes, this was the third in the *Goo* series, which, perhaps, sums up the twentieth century. Future historians, probing the rubble of ancient Hollywood for our age's counterparts of stone tablets, for the antiquities of our constipated culture, may well find *Return of the Ghost of the Creeping Goo* and say, "Urp."

Jeremy Slade, like King Kong — who dreamed of Queen Kong — had a dream. He wanted to make a billion dollars. And, obviously, he didn't give a hoot how he made it. He was, so far, just a little more than a billion dollars short of his goal.

Here's what happened. Slade made *The Creeping Goo*, in which Goo died. On its release to theaters the plot repeated itself like a sour stomach, and Goo also died in the theaters. Nothing daunted, or else absolutely out of his mind, Slade made *Ghost of the Creeping Goo*, despite expensive delays during its shooting. After lying as if dead for the first two weeks after release, something happened; the picture came alive; it hit a nerve.

People started paying money to see it. Lots of people, and big money. So, in response to popular psychosis — and in a frenzy of greed — Slade had embarked upon this kookie epic. Now, on this splendidly sunshiny Southern California morning, Thursday, the twenty-third of April, Slade was seventeen days into his twenty-one-day shooting schedule, and smack on the budget.

I could hear Phrye saying, "Well, it looked good, we'll print that one. Let's get set up for the rescue bit."

Next to me, tall, handsome, superbly muscled Ed Howell, male star of this crime against humanity, said, "Pretty good, hey, Shell?"

I turned and grinned at him. "Yeah. If you refer to the fleeing tomato. But if you mean eight-foot oysters and monster beetles — "

"Who said anything about beetles?" Ed's grin flashed in his black face.

He was one of the finest actors in Hollywood, or points east for that matter, but this was his first starring role — and better than a bit part somewhere else, at that Wearing only a white loincloth studded with gold sequins, he looked like a Greek god carved from living ebony. He was pretty dark-skinned to begin with, but the make-up department had smeared him with some kind of black gunk that gleamed in the sunlight — because the locale of all three *Goo* films was Venus. And, as nearly everybody knows by now, of the five Venusian races, the ruling race is *really* black.

While we'd been standing here together a number of not-quite-startled glances had been aimed our way. Which didn't surprise me, not only because this was my first visit to the *Goo* location, since I'm not an actor — though I'd often thought hamming it up a little might be fun — but because it sometimes happens even when I'm standing alone.

In the first place, all by myself I'm six feet, two inches tall and weigh two hundred and six pounds; Ed was an inch taller, and together we'd bend the scale at four-twenty. Even though he was a Negro, his skin wasn't a hell of a lot darker than mine, since I get a lot of sun and am tanned the approximate shade of a pale Watusi. But where his hair was abundant, black, full over the ears and at the back of his head, mine is nearly as white as sheets bleached in new improved Bleacho, is cut about an inch long, and sticks straight up into the air as if magnetized and repelled by my scalp.

Even adding white eyebrows over gray eyes, the brows angling up and out from the middle and then swooping down sharply at the ends, the sort of dashingly broken nose, and the hardly noticeable bit trimmed from my left ear by a poorly aimed bullet, and the extremely fine and faint scar over my right eye, there isn't anything really distressing about me. I like to think. But, still, I've had a few of those looks. As if I were some kind of subversive, undermining beauty.

I suppose, though, I might have gawked a bit myself at the sight of Ed and me together. Besides the obvious points of contrast, I had some clothes on. Where Ed merely wore that gold-sequined loincloth, I was resplendent in a new suit, superbly tailored if I do say so myself, in a basic shade of blue which sort of rippled and changed to include tints of gold and maybe a little purple and even green — one of those iridescent fabrics that shimmer chameleon-like in the sunlight. True, the last time I'd worn it a disgruntled mobster had told me I looked like a living fungus; but what would a disgruntled mobster know about jazzy apparel? I liked to think of myself in the suit merely as sort of radiantly glowing.

So, radiantly glowing in the sunlight, I said to Ed, "O.K., except for the oysters, and beetles, and Goo, and the men, it's great. When do you get to rescue Cherry and breathe fire and waggle your muscles and — "

He waggled his muscles. "Soon as they set up. Few minutes now."

"I gather she leaps into the drink, then you plow through the oysters and jump into the flaming glop. And save her, naturally."

"Naturally. I'm very good at the brave stuff. But I do hate the thought of getting burned to death. Hope they get it in one take."

"They will."

He grinned, and I grinned back at him. We both knew — I'd think by now the whole movie-going world would know — that neither Slade nor Phrye were exactly what you'd call perfectionists. They weren't exactly what you'd call careful. They were lousy. If an actor goofed and referred to Lillian Cerulean as Loolian, they merely added a line to a later scene: ". . . So I spoke to Lillian — or, as she is sometimes called, Loolian."

However, despite a flaw here and there — and there — and there — Slade's movies had something for everybody; lovelies for the men, handsome Ed Howell and John Brick for the ladies, a cliff-hanger plot for the kids, and monsters for the nuts. And, always, there were very shapely tomatoes, who raced about wearing nightgowns in broad daylight and falling into water. It is perhaps a flaw in my otherwise sterling character, but I greatly enjoy those scenes in movies when shapely tomatoes race about in nightgowns and fall into water.

"Well, I better get over there, Shell," Ed said.

"Be brave."

"Are you kidding?" He walked toward the cameras and equipment now set up near the cliff's edge.

In a minute I lit a cigarette and headed that way myself. Might as well get a good look at the heroics. And, of course, the falling into water.

This, in case it needs to be said, was not my usual occupation. My usual occupation is chief of staff, and staff, of *Sheldon Scott, Investigations*, the office up one flight in the Hamilton Building between Third and Fourth Streets in downtown Los Angeles, on which I pay the rent.

I was, actually, hard at work earning the rent money, and perhaps you can now understand why I love my work. When the job started, I'd had no idea I would be eyeballing monsters and vitamin-packed tomatoes; it had started out like a routine investigation — then suddenly there was blood seeping from a dead man's head, and hard-faced hoods prowling about, and my client was in the can booked on suspicion of murder. Part of that suspicion was mine, because there seemed a good chance my client was, indeed, a murderer most foul. And if he was, he was going to become a headless murderer most foul, because I intended to knock his block off.

In the meantime, I was here on the *Goo* set for a few words with Natasha Antoinette, the thirty-nine-inch star of the movie — that doesn't mean she was a midget, by the way. However, I'd been forbidden by producer Slade to talk to the gal, and possibly upset her more than she was usually upset on the set, which was quite a lot, until her upcoming scene was completed.

She was pretty high-strung to begin with, but she had more reason to be nervous than most. Negro actors and actresses often had bit parts or good supporting roles in Hollywood films, but rarely if ever did they star in them. At least not in "white" movies. For Natasha, as for Ed Howell, this was her first starring role, and she was understandably anxious about it.

The upcoming scene was referred to hereabouts as the "death dance," and Natasha was supposed to wiggle sinuously for hairy John Brick, who was playing the part of Gruzakk, a kind of latter-day Venusian Genghis Khan. He was the leader of a band of white bandits who had captured the black Queen of Venus, Natasha, and who were going to wreak all sorts of vengeance upon her. If Natasha's dance annoyed Gruzakk, she got her head chopped off; if it pleased him, she got raped. It was a moot question which was the worse fate, but, I thought, it should be fun to watch. Especially if she pleased Gruzakk.

The area chosen by Slade for his "Venusian" landscape was two hundred acres or so of a farm a few miles north of Hollywood owned by a retired movie actress named Madelyn Willow, and it was possible it looked a good deal like Venus, since nobody — nobody of my acquaintance anyway — had ever seen Venus up close. At least there was a fine cliff below which had been constructed the artificial lake, on which oil could be poured and ignited to make quite a lot of fire and dark smoke bubble up from the water's surface; also there were a few hills about, or rather mounds of earth, up and down which the various outsized creepies could gallop in hot pursuit of the black, white, brown, yellow, and green — in descending pecking order — female Venusians. Naturally, with all those pretty skins, plus fire and smoke and monsters, the film was being shot in Lividcolor.

If Slade's production company had operated with the care and precision of most other outfits, it would have been tomorrow before I could have talked to Natasha, if then. First the rescue of Cherry had to be filmed, and ordinarily half a dozen takes of the rescue scene might have been shot before the crew moved on to Natasha's death dance. But not with Slade and Phrye in control.

When two cameras had been moved in near the cliff's edge and another below close to the lake, final readings taken by the camera operators on their light meters, last touches completed by make-up men and dressers, a mike boom poised to catch Cherry's last scream, and the assistant director hoarse from yelling, "*Quiet!*", Phrye called, "All right, let's shoot it Roll . . . action!" — and it was all over two minutes later.

Cherry spun and leaped from the cliff, choosing to be burned to death rather than digested alive, and began splashing about. From nowhere appeared big Ed Howell, brandishing an enormous aluminum sword. Hack, slash, crunch, and three oysters lay clacking their last. Ed dived from the cliff, cut the water cleanly, and swam toward Cherry, pushing the water ahead of him with a modified breast stroke to keep the flames away. It isn't too difficult to swim in water covered with flaming oil, but it's not a pastime for the faint hearted. Nothing went wrong, however, and in another minute Ed had reached the shore and was carrying Cherry's limp form toward a patch of green under a prop-department tree with leaves like opened umbrellas. As he placed her on the grass, Phrye allowed as to how that one looked good, and they'd print it. One take. Next, Natasha's dance.

I found a Fiberglas rock and sat on it. In a few minutes Ed and Cherry strolled up from the lake below, wet and somewhat bedraggled, but without blisters. Ed waved and went on toward Phrye, but Cherry walked over and stopped by me and my rock.

I stood up. I'd talked to Cherry for a few minutes earlier this morning, and now she said, "I see you're still here, Shell."

"I told you I wouldn't miss your big scene."

"How was I?"

"Magnificent. Then, and now."

It was true, without any exaggeration. Maybe she hadn't had real opportunity for Academy Award-type emoting, but she got the Shell Scott Award. Her beige-blonde hair was darker now, heavy with water, but the dampness couldn't dim the brightness of those blue eyes and it sure hadn't lessened the stimulating impact of her outfit.

They didn't wear any underthings on Venus. Didn't wear much overthings, either. The thin cloth clung to her firm healthy young body as if alive and with a sneaky mind of its own, a transparent covering more provocative than nudity. I pulled my eyes back up to her face but it didn't help much. Those smiling red lips looked as if they'd been expelled from kissing school. But not for playing hooky.

"What are you thinking?" Cherry asked me.

She was still smiling so apparently she didn't know. And I wasn't going to tell her, either. Instead I said, with remarkable stupidity, "Oh, just . . . thoughts."

"Thinking thoughts?"

"Yes. I do it often when I think."

"How clever."

"You're very kind. And astute. And gorgeous. Hoo — "

Cherry colored slightly but prettily, possibly because of my comments or possibly because of the way my eyes were rolling, and then she tried to cover herself with her hands, but she didn't have enough hands.

"Well," she said, "I have to go change."

"Change?"

"Get out of these wet clothes."

"Ah, yes."

"And into some dry ones, of course."

"Of course. You'd hardly get into more wet ones, would you? Is there anything I — "

"No. You'd peek."

"I suppose I would. How did you know?"

"Because you've been peeking. Bye. See you later, Shell."

She walked past me and undulated away toward the parking lot. Yeah, the parking lot. That's where her dressing room was. Her car was her dressing room. You've heard of the producer who spared no expense to keep his crew feeling happy and loved and well adjusted? Jeremy Slade wasn't him.

You couldn't blame Slade too much, though. He was working on a very tight and not magnificent budget. Moreover, he'd gotten stuck for a wad while making *Ghost of the Creeping Goo* when one of his female leads flipped out of the picture for two or three weeks; there'd even been rumors Slade was on the edge of going broke. But he'd managed to scrape enough loot together to keep going — and now it looked as if the film, which he'd managed to salvage and complete, would make a packet.

The parking lot was about two hundred yards from where the current scenes were being shot, and I naturally watched Cherry walking away. Then I heard Phrye yelling.

There was what appeared to be total confusion for a while — men moving cameras, reflectors, electrical cable, booms; setting up a couple of high-powered lamps — but in a remarkably short time the movement slowed and nearly stopped, the apparent confusion having been merely the efficient preparations of a well trained and experienced crew.

"All right, shut up," Phrye yelled. "Shut *up!* Dammit, we're making a picture here, dammit. Shut up, *quiet!*"

The star, Natasha Antoinette, stood a little apart from the others, reading a newspaper. I'd moved up to stand a few yards behind Phrye. Slade was near him, and Natasha was only about five yards away on my left. I thought I saw her sway slightly, like a slim dark tree in a wind.

"Places," Phrye called. "Get with it. Natasha? Where in hell's Natasha?"

She'd been reading something on the newspaper's front page, apparently the right-hand column. She slowly moistened a finger and started to turn the page, but didn't turn it. Instead, she fainted.

I guess she fainted. At least she went down like a stone. She was so close to me and fell so limply that I heard her head thump dully as it hit the earth. It made a sound like a man banging the heels of his hands together. She lay still.

She was still, but suddenly there was a lot of other movement. Half a dozen men started toward her almost simultaneously. Jeremy Slade was the first to reach her, Ed Howell close behind him, then Walter Phrye. Then me. Maybe I'd still been thinking about Cherry. If you want the truth, I *had* still been thinking about Cherry. Anyhow, I wasn't as alert as usual. By the time I got next to her, Natasha's eyelids were fluttering and the corners of her mouth were twitching as if she were spasmodically attempting to smile. But I've seen men shot in the stomach grimace the same way, and they weren't smiling, either. Besides, she wasn't even conscious yet, just starting to come back to the world.

It took four or five minutes before she got all the way back. "It's nothing," she was saying. "Really. I just felt suddenly faint. . . . And everything . . . went away." She paused, then went on. "I'm all right now. I — haven't been eating breakfast. Dieting. Probably I'm just hungry. I'm all right."

Her voice, always soft, was like two shreds of velvet rubbing together. Then she smiled, the slow, brilliant, beautiful smile for which she was famous — one of the things for which she was famous — apparently back to normal once more. But her eyes still wobbled a little.

Slade looked pretty sick himself. If his star conked out on him now, he'd be in a pickle. He licked dry lips, caressed Natasha's brown arm with a rough hand. "You O.K., baby? You sure you're O.K.?" His voice was high, thin, and fluting. But, then, it always was.

She seemed to shrink from him, pulling her arm away.

"I'm fine, Jerry. Just give me a minute, will you?"

"All the time you want, sweetheart. You'll be able to do the dance, won't you? Think you'll be able to do the dance?"

"I'll do it. I'll do it, Jerry."

The newspaper she'd been reading was spread out at her feet. It was this morning's L.A. *Herald-Standard*, but that was all I noticed before someone picked it up and crumpled it. The crowd bunched around us began milling slowly, starting to break up. Cameramen and technicians went back to the set. In a few more minutes the actors and actresses — including Natasha — were in their places, action about to start.

And while waiting for the cameras to start rolling I wondered, among other things, if Natasha Antoinette might really have had a big, filling, nutritious breakfast this morning.

I knew Natasha and liked her — in fact, she and Ed Howell had joined me and a giddy redheaded tomato at my Hollywood apartment a few weeks back, for an evening of highballs and hamburgers, and we'd all gotten along marvelously well. True, Nat was a very high-strung gal, but one thing she didn't look was undernourished. That night, for example, she'd eaten three hamburgers. With onions.

Besides, there was that phone call last night. The call and what had followed it — which was what I wanted to ask her about. The sniffling woman on the phone had *said* she was Natasha Antoinette, but I didn't have any proof it had really been Nat.

More, Gordon Waverly had also said he hadn't killed anybody — and just possibly he'd been lying. If so, maybe *I* was in a pickle. Because Gordon Waverly was my client. And somebody had indubitably been killed. Very messily, quite positively, killed.

So as Walter Phrye called out, "All right, ready, everybody? Roll . . .", I thought about all that. About last night, and Natasha, and Gordon Waverly. And murder. And, of course, the hard-faced hoodlums, alive and dead. . . .

Two

This was a grand night for it, I thought.

A grand night for gently stirred Martinis and charcoaled steaks — rare — and maybe a little wine with the steaks — red wine, to match the steaks, and the rare wine-red lips of the lass sitting on the chocolate-brown divan in my apartment, number 212 in Hollywood's Spartan Apartment Hotel.

I'd spent the day in my L.A. office downtown, watching the fish — guppies, in a ten-gallon tank atop the bookcase — and reading Emerson, and waiting for the silent phone to ring, which it didn't. I'm a man who requires action to use up the thyroxin, or pituitrin, or twitches, or whatever builds up in me while I'm idle, so when the phone continued not to ring, I used it myself — to call the lass now sitting on my chocolate-brown divan.

The compact Japanese brazier was chock-full of charcoal, sitting in the middle of my yellow-gold carpet, and I had already doused the coals with fire-starting juice but had not yet held a match to the concoction. The living-room windows were open — because this was an experiment, and the way I cook it was conceivable that something might go wrong, like my burning down the apartment and the rest of the block — the first Martinis were mixed, the lass was smiling, and all seemed in readiness.

She said, "Shell, do you really think this will work?"

"Who knows? We have adequate ventilation. We have charcoal. We have booze and wine and steaks. And even if all that goes to pot, we have you and me. How can we lose?"

"But . . . won't it be smoky?"

"Perhaps," I said mysteriously. "Perhaps not." I spoke mysteriously because it was a big mystery to me. I didn't have the faintest idea. I had never tried charcoaling steaks in my living room before; but picnic spots are hard to find in the heart of the L.A.-Hollywood cement. The green grounds and fairways of the Wilshire Country Club, directly across North Rossmore from the Spartan, would have been dandy; but even the *members* can't light fires on the Wilshire Country Club grounds and fairways.

"The only way to find out," I said, "is to find out. What if the Wright brothers had sat around saying to each other, 'Brother, do you think it will fly?' What if Papa Dionne had said 'Fooey?' What if — "

"Oh, Shell."

"There are risks in practically everything, my sweet. That's what makes life exciting. Isn't this exciting?"

"Not very. I'm hungry."

She was dampening my ardor. She was a model, and this was our first date, and she was gorgeous, but she was dampening my ardor. She didn't wear a brassiere; she wore a living blouse; still, she was dampening my ardor.

I said, "You won't feel so hungry after we've eaten. Neither will I, for that matter. It's a simple matter of mathematics — "

"Light it, will you?"

The damned woman was taking all the fun out of cooking. And I don't much like cooking to begin with. The hell with her and her living blouse.

"O.K.," I said glumly. "But anticipation is sometimes greater than realization, and I have the feeling it will be much more fun anticipating *this* meal than — "

"*Light* it, will you?"

Well, the time had come. I guess that, subconsciously, I'd been dreading it. I squatted over the coals and lit a match. It was a moment of some suspense.

The phone rang.

"Huh," I said.

"Well, answer it."

"I'm afraid to."

"Don't be silly."

"I mean, it might be — oh, somebody murdered or something. Then I'd have to leave this gay party."

"Don't be silly."

The phone rang again.

"Shell, answer it. I'm *hungry*."

I answered the phone.

Sounds of a fish dying in a pool. Sniffling and snuffling, moist sounds.

"Hello?" I said again.

"Is this Mr. Scott?"

"Yeah. What's — who's calling?"

"Shell? Is it you?"

"Hell, yes, it's me. Who else? So what's the matter?" I wasn't at my amiable best.

"Good. This is Nat."

"Who?" It didn't register right away.

"Nat — Natasha Antoinette."

"Ah. Yes." It registered.

Beauteous film star, bit parts and then second leads, and lately femme lead in a monstrosity called *Ghost of the Creeping Goo*. But a stunning gal. Especially after falling into water.

"He*ll*o, Nat," I said, at my amiable best. "What can I do for you?"

"It's not me, Shell. I just wanted to be sure it was you. Mr. Waverly wants to talk to you."

"Not you?"

She was gone. Then a man spoke to my ear. "This is Gordon Waverly, Mr. Scott."

"So?" I was a bit disgruntled. The good-looking women seemed to be getting away from me tonight. Maybe it was one of those nights when the planets form malefic aspects and shoot poisoned darts at you. "What happened to Natasha Antoinette?" I said.

"She is right here beside me, Mr. Scott. It is primarily because of her that I am calling. Ah . . ." He hesitated. "I would prefer not to explain everything over the phone. Could you come to my office tonight?"

It was nine P.M. Chow time. Martini time. Lass on the divan time. I said, "Right now?"

"If it is convenient, sir. I'd like for you to conduct an investigation for me. There may be nothing . . . ah, there may be little to my suspicions. But, on the other hand, if they are well founded, this could be a very grave matter, of the greatest urgency." He paused. "Perhaps my name means nothing to you, Mr. Scott. I am the publisher of *Inside* magazine."

That rang a bell. *Inside* was a two-year-old weekly slanted for the movie and television industry, and now ranked right up there with *Variety* and the *Hollywood Reporter*. You just weren't with it in Hollywood unless you could quote the latest news or quips or barbs from *Inside*. And Gordon Waverly, because of his position as its publisher, was one of the most influential men in the tinsel town. He was on a first-name basis with many of the great and near-great of Hollywood, had entree to the homes of producers, stars, top-dogs, and bottom dogs. If he had trouble for which he might require a detective's services, it was probably interesting trouble.

I said, "Can you give me an idea what the problem is, Mr. Waverly?"

"I would prefer to tell you in person. This — well, if what Miss Antoinette has just told me is true, we may be on the verge of an enormous scandal in Hollywood. Enormous. I would much prefer that you meet me here, if it is at all possible, sir." He paused, and then went on again. "Oh, I shall gladly pay your usual fee. And I now guarantee you a minimum fee of one thousand dollars, merely to hear my story and conduct a brief preliminary investigation. Assuming you can come to my office immediately. Can you, Mr. Scott?"

I looked at the unlighted charcoal. At the undrunk Martinis. At the lass on my chocolate-brown divan.

She said, "Hurry up. I'm *hungry*."

That did it. "You," I said grimly, "are going to get a mite *hung*rier." Then into the phone's mouthpiece I said, "Sure, Mr. Waverly. I've a — chore to take care of first, but I'll be with you in half an hour."

"That will be satisfactory, sir. I'll have a check waiting for you upon your arrival." We hung up.

The gal was scowling. Or pouting, or breaking up. Doing something unappetizing with her face, anyway. "Well, hell," I said. "You told me to answer it."

Three

The offices of *Inside* are on Hollywood Boulevard east of Vine, about a block past the big Paramount Theater building. I found a parking spot across the street, climbed out of my sky-blue Cadillac convertible, and stood next to it waiting for a break in the traffic.

While preparing to jaywalk, I glanced at the pink face of the *Inside* building. It looked as if it were blushing — as well it might. I gazed across the width of "glamorous" Hollywood Boulevard at the blushing-pink façade of the *Inside* building, and wondered. Wondered, as I sometimes do, about "Hollywood." And also wondered — with, I'll admit, some anticipation — what I was getting into this time.

It could be nothing — or anything.

Weird things happen in Hollywood. Errant twitches gather in high-powered noodles and on occasion erupt into mania. We natives live in the midst of controlled madness, on the thin edge of convulsion. It could hardly be otherwise. People who sell dreams have to expect to buy a few nightmares.

But more. Hollywood has been described as a state of mind, and if so it's a state that hasn't quite been admitted to the Union. It's a dream world with make-believe boundaries, an Idea of ideas, a rainbow-colored aura-in-the-round, an invisible cloud of thought — billions of old and new thoughts, bright and dull ones, cold and hot ones, lurking in and above the city's physical body. It's the city of "everyday people," and also of everything from born geniuses to self-made bastards, a place where you can peel off make-up and get down to the real make-up; and it is also the continual paradox — like my standing on "glamorous" drab Hollywood Boulevard, outside *Inside* — a never-never land where it's always always. "I'll love you always," "You'll always be with Magna Pix, doll," "I always said you'd be bigger than Valentine, sweetheart," — and "always" means "at least till tomorrow, baby."

It's the land of the false front and the falsie and even the detachable behind, where you knock on a door and open it to find yourself staring at the Hollywood Hills, where the Oscar should be made of foam rubber and candlelit cleavage. A land of magnificence, and soaring talent, and gorgeous flesh and fire and magnetism; but also of the tall children, the frauds and phonies, the weepers, and the creeps. It is also a land where the knives drip honey and the guillotine hides behind smiling lips. Maybe it's only a little different from Chicago, or New York, or Philadelphia, Pa., but that little goes a long long way; they bite in all those places, too, but in Hollywood the teeth are sharper.

Some of the sharpest teeth in the entire U.S. of A. were affixed to the pink gums of *Inside*.

Not that the writers who phrased news and columns for the weekly were vicious or sadistic. Not that at all. They were simply bright and clever and very truthful. And truth is sharper than knives and needles; it can cut deeper than the quick — especially can it cut, and wound, those who have had little acquaintance with it.

Needless to say, into that category fell many who dwelled in "Hollywood." Why not? Many whose careers consisted of pretending to be somebody else — in a play, a movie, a TV segment — kept on pretending after working hours; they might be Casanova or Marie Antoinette for a month — then, for six months, Rasputin or Saint Joan. Some of them never did learn who they were; some of them didn't care. Some of them lived their shadowy roles so well that they became impotent or frigid while playing a eunuch or a nun, and hell on springs while starring as a libertine or a bawd. Much of Hollywood's "scandal" was the result less of weakness or design than of words typed on yellow paper by professional scribblers and lived too well by professional pretenders.

And these were the people who, every Monday, devoured — and sometimes were devoured by — *Inside*.

Engrossed in my idle thoughts I had somehow managed to stroll idly across Hollywood Boulevard without suffering a broken neck. Something, I sometimes think, watches over me. My good fairy, maybe. Whatever it is, I now stood before a building in which it looked as if several good fairies might happily abide: the bottom floor of the Garrison Building, filling half a block from left to right before me; mostly glass — with a faint pinkish tint — and a kind of foamy pink molding at its top like frosting on a big rectangular cupcake; gauzy draperies inside the glass walls, just thick enough so passersby couldn't peep in at the *Insiders* working like beavers.

You almost imagined the staff in there clad in veils and berets and dirndls, dancing around a candy-striped maypole. It looked *so* harmless. It made me think of Mrs. Dillinger saying, "John's such a *sweet* child," or of Jack the Ripper in knee pants.

It was nine-thirty-five P.M. I'd made good time, considering the ten minutes I'd had to spend telling my date that business should come before pleasure, duty before dissipation, virtue before vice; that my business and duty and virtue — and livelihood — reposed in my answering the calls of citizens in distress, day or night, like a kindly old country doctor; and that, dammit, she'd asked for it.

Nonetheless, when I left her she had retained on her face an expression as though something she'd eaten with joy and anticipation lay souring in her pretty tummy, refusing utterly to digest. But I knew that couldn't have been it and for a guilty moment I thought of her sitting, grimacing, listening to her stomach growling; but then I cast guilt and the past behind me and forged ahead. Into the future. Into *Inside*.

They were swinging doors. Not the kind that close with a *pssss* of compressed air, but those that waggle back and forth, gently, to a stop. They swung almost silently shut behind me, with only a little *poof, poof, pooh-pooh-poo* of wind.

A blonde puff of peaches and cream and the kind of bosom displayed in bosom-building advertisements as an example of what *can* happen, sat behind a fragile-looking pink desk on my right. An empty desk was opposite her, and at the rear of the room a carpeted hallway led left and right to hidden offices. The walls were papered with something glittery, bearing a faint design which appeared to be ghostly gazelles and unicorns leaping about in passionate frolic. Indirect lighting suffused the air with a soft, pleasant glow. With incense burning, and a big brass gong hanging in the corner, it would have been a great room for an orgy.

I merely glanced at all that, then returned my attention to the blonde. Secretaries and receptionists are often either very decorative or very efficient, but not often both at once. I played a little game with myself, trying to guess which this one was. And it didn't take me any time at all to find out.

She said, "Helloo-o," in a voice like doves making up, then added, "Are you Mr. Scott?"

"You bet I am."

"Here." She handed me a slip of paper.

It was a check for one thousand dollars. Waverly sure hadn't been kidding when he'd said he would have a check "waiting for me." I pocketed it with mild misgivings. I didn't like getting my hands on a retainer until and unless I'd definitely taken a case. Which I hadn't done yet — not quite. But I figured I could hash that out with Gordon Waverly himself.

The blonde just sat there batting her eyes at me, so I said, "I have an appointment with Mr. Waverly."

"He isn't here. He — " She hesitated. "He left in quite a hurry. Just — suddenly raced out."

"Oh? Did he say I should wait here for him, or what?"

"Well, he didn't say. Shortly after nine he buzzed me and said to expect a Mr. Scott in about half an hour. And to have that check ready for you. Then a few minutes ago he just left his office and went out past me. Shouting. Quite rapidly."

"Shouting quite rapidly?"

"No." She smiled dreamily. "Went *out* quite rapidly."

"Uh-huh. Fine. What was he shouting?"

"'Finley Pike! I'll fix that Finley Pike!' It gave me quite a startle."

"I'll bet it diddle. Now, what is a finleypike?"

"Mr. Pike. Mr. Finley Pike. He's one of our vice presidents. He works for *Inside*."

"Ah. And Mr. Waverly said he was going to fix him."

"Shouted. He shouted it. Then raced out."

Well, we were getting somewhere. Muddle was coming out of confusion. Maybe I was learning why *Inside* wasn't a daily.

"Can you add anything helpful, ma'am? Like, did he shout anything else? Was he carrying a naked sword, or a wrench, or anything? Did he say what, or how, or why he was going to fix Mr. Pike? Was he alone? In the midst of a crowd — "

"It was just as I told you. And of course he wasn't in a mist of a crowd."

"Wasn't a woman here? Natasha Antoinette, perhaps?"

"No, he was alone. At least when he ran out. Why did you mention Natasha Antoinette?"

"I thought she was with Mr. Waverly when he phoned me."

"I wouldn't know about that. I was just sitting here. When Mr. Waverly works late, he keeps me on handy, in case he wants . . . like to dictate letters or find something in the files, or . . . Like that. Someone *might* have been with him — they don't have to come in the front-door entrance."

"Well, since Mr. Waverly left no instructions for me, I'll take independent action. Like trying to find him. Would you give me Mr. Pike's address?"

Zip, she punched a button on a little box, and something flipped up, and she said, "It's twenty-two-seventeen Gable Avenue." She was efficient too. "That's north of Hollywood, up in the hills a little," she said.

"I'll find it. Thank you, ma'am."

"It's miss, not ma'am. You're welcome."

"Thanks."

We seemed to have gotten that backward, but in this heady atmosphere it somehow seemed right. I left. The doors sighed, *pooh-pooh-poo*, behind me.

Four

It was only about a mile to Finley Pike's address. Down Hollywood Boulevard to Gable, then straight up the tree-lined road to the twenty-two-hundred block. But well before I got there it became apparent that more than Gordon Waverly was ahead of me.

A police cruiser sat at the curb, red light pulsing above its windshield. Another radio car was parked in a white cement driveway next to a brown frame house. I couldn't see the number yet, but I had a hunch it would be 2217. More than a hunch. Lights were on over the front doors of nearby houses, and knots of people huddled together on the sidewalks.

I didn't like it. The people who thus spontaneously gather seldom gather to beam upon young lovers, or ex-caterpillars testing iridescent wings, or birds' beaks cracking small blue eggs, or any kind of lovely or happy thing; they swarm to fire and disaster, gaze entranced at gruesome messes, and especially are they drawn to mayhem and destruction, the dead and the dying. No, I didn't like it at all. It was as if, with a kind of psychic nostril, I could smell blood. And the back of my neck got a little colder, just a little.

Because I was thinking these somewhat uncharitable thoughts, the other car almost slammed into me. It was a big black Imperial sedan, coming like a singed bat out of hell toward me from my left. I was starting into the intersection when the flare of its lights hit my eyes.

I snapped my head left, then yanked the steering wheel and hit the brakes, skidded, tugged the wheel back just before banging into the curb. The Imperial was swinging left into Gable, tires shrieking as they slipped sideways on the asphalt, now skidding almost parallel to me. I fought the wheel and at the same time managed one quick glimpse at the other car — and in the fractional moment somehow saw, and recognized, two faces.

Both faces were turned toward me, mouths open and eyes probably as wide as my own, features twisted in sudden alarm. But I made them both. There were other guys in the back of the Imperial, but these two men were in the front seat, the guy nearer to me a slick-fingered ex-cannon who, unlike most others of his trade, had switched from boosting wallets and jools to squeezing the trigger of a .45-caliber banger, and the other — in the driver's seat — a well-nigh brainless wheelman who, despite his paucity of other talents, could drive a car clear around the Indianapolis Speedway, through traffic, backwards, without scraping a fender.

He didn't even scrape the fender of my Cad, which was at least a minor miracle. Both cars came to shuddering stops. The Imperial was sideways in the middle of the street, and my Cad was to its right, almost touching the curb. I moved. Without thinking — at least without conscious thought.

I knew there was some kind of trouble close ahead, and I also knew those two faces belonged to hoods who themselves belonged to an enormously tough customer named Al Gant, and I knew very well that Al Gant would cheerfully haul out my guts and wrap them around my neck and strangle me with them, should the opportunity ever arise.

But that awareness was only in the back of my head if anywhere in it, and I simply slapped the Cad's gears into low and pulled ahead until I was in front of the other car, blocking it. Then I got out and stepped over to the Imperial, leaned on the open window, and eyeballed the pockmarked face of J. B. Kester, usually called J. B., ex-pickpocket turned killer.

"Hello, J. B.," I said. "Al send you?"

"Al who?"

"Capone, of course. Hell, Al Gant."

"Al? You got rocks in your head, Scott. We're just — just drivin' around lookin' for girls."

I had to laugh. "Sure. I can see you, drinking beer and whistling at the skirts. What's all the excitement here at Pike's? Al send you to kill somebody?"

I bent my knees a bit and peered past J. B. at broad, heavy, fat-faced Joe "Mooneyes" Garella. Ordinarily a hood with a name like that would have been called Joe Gorilla, but "Mooneyes" was a natural tag for this slow and sluglike citizen. His face was pinker than *Inside*'s outside, and except for a small squashed nose and fat red lips and wisps of red hair in disarray on his scalp, his face seemed mostly eyes. Two large, blank, watery, and lashless eyes paler than fog at dawn dominated his face, seemed to possess it. He looked like a guy turning into an owl.

"Hi, Mooneyes," I said. "Where's the fire? Who're you supposed to burn?"

"Scott, damn your guts," J. B. said, not pleasantly, "can the stool. I told you — "

"Yeah, girls."

But he wasn't listening. The whole gang in the car seemed only now to have become aware of the commotion directly ahead of us. The knots of people. The cars. The red lights flashing. In a word: *cops!*

"Fuzz!" squawked J. B. He jabbed a thumb into Mooneyes' ribs, and almost before I could move my feet so they wouldn't get run over, the car had been swung back in a speedy arc, forward in a reverse arc, and was purring off the way it had come.

Here in a hurry. Gone in a hurry. And all of them Al Gant's boys. Something for me to think about — but not at the moment. I started the Cad and moved it ahead a few yards, parked at the curb opposite the scene of the commotion. The number was 2217, all right.

As I got out of the car a spot of white ahead of the right front fender caught my eye. It lay in the street, a foot or two out from the curb. Anything fluttering about at "the scene of the crime" may be worth picking up, and I was by now at least half convinced this was the scene of some kind of violation more serious than spitting on the sidewalk. So I picked it up.

It looked like a page from a letter, but when I'd read a few lines I began wondering if it might not be, instead, part of the first draft of a story for *True Agony Confessions* Magazine. Written by an idiot. To be read by people who gather in knots at mayhems.

The part my eye fell on was kind of interesting. It was near the bottom of the sheet: ". . . knocked up with a pregnancy right there on his damn couch! Anyways so I had the kid and he dont know it yet. Should I tell him? I cant help it bothering me some. Maybe he ought to be told but he don't deserve no special considerations the way I see it. But of course I kept the money for the abortion. But I never had no idea when I went for help — help! ha-ha! — to Dr. Willim — " And that was the end of the page.

Al Gant's boys. Now this. But first, whatever was going on across the street.

At the entrance, broad shoulders blocking the door, was a ham-handed and rock-muscled police sergeant named Ken Carver. A solid, dependable, quiet-talking policeman, comfortable and competent in his job. In the vernacular, "a good cop" — but most of them are.

He raised a thick eyebrow when he saw me. "Boy, you got a nose like an anteater, Scott. How'd you smell this one?"

"I didn't, Ken. I was — well, I guess I was hired by Mr. Gordon Waverly earlier — "

"For what?"

I shook my head. "I don't actually know yet. All I know is, I was to meet him at his office, learned he'd come here, and came here myself to find him. Maybe you can tell me."

"Maybe. Gordon Waverly, huh? You guess you were hired by him? You don't know?"

"Not exactly."

"Well, you better make up your mind exactly." Ken jerked a thumb. "He's inside. Looks like he killed a guy named Finley Pike."

Five

It looked like it, all right.

Because I knew Ken and was also a long-time friend of Lieutenant Bill Rawlins, who was inside the house, I was permitted go in and look around.

One thing was certain. If the guy on the floor was Finley Pike, Finley Pike was dead.

The little man sprawled face down on the carpet might have had a good head of hair earlier this evening, but now it was a head of blood and bone and pulpy pinkish-grayness. Several feet from the body a marble or ivory idol lay in a small spot of stickiness.

Nothing had been moved yet; the Crime Lab crew had just arrived from SID. A technician was dusting for prints, and Rawlins was standing on my right talking to a man seated in a purple overstuffed chair. The man was lean, tanned, with a sharp-boned, almost stern face, gray hair brushed straight back over his head and full at the temples.

We'd never met, but most of Hollywood knew that face: Gordon Waverly. My client. Or, rather: my client? It remained to be seen.

A flashbulb popped as the police photographer shot another picture, and in the glare I saw a thin curving line of red on the side of Waverly's head, running down below the gray at his temple.

After ushering me inside, Ken had gone over to speak with Rawlins. Now the lieutenant glanced around, then said something to Waverly and walked across the room to me.

"Hi, Shell. What's this Ken tells me about you and Waverly? Are you or aren't you working for the guy?"

I grinned. "Ken knows nearly as much as I do, Bill." I told him about talking to Waverly on the phone and added, "I checked his office and was told he'd come here. So I buzzed out myself. That's it."

"Interesting. You don't know what he wanted you to do?"

"Nope. Something about the possibility of a big scandal, that's all. Too hush-hush for the phone, I gathered."

"Well, *this* is going to be a pretty good scandal. Hardly seems likely he'd try to get you on his side and then come here and kill this guy."

"Hardly. Did he kill Pike?"

"Not much doubt about that. When we got here the victim was — " he nodded toward Pike's body — "like that, where he is now. Waverly was conscious, on his feet, standing looking down at him."

"Don't tell me he was clutching the murder weapon and — "

Rawlins cut me off with a grin. "No, not much doubt that idol caved in Pike's skull. But it was lying where it is now, several feet from the victim's body. Waverly claims he was knocked out and came to there where the idol is, right next to it. Barely got to his feet when we came in. Says he must have been clubbed with the thing, too."

"What else does he say?"

"That's about it. Came here to see Pike, no answer, door was unlocked, and he walked in. Saw Pike on the floor, and a leather case — attaché case, he thinks — open near him. Filled with some kind of papers."

"Just some kind? Or was he more specific?"

"He doesn't know what kind, just papers. He walked over to Pike and bent down by him, and boom. Slugged. That's all he knows — except he didn't do it. At least that's his story."

"He say what he wanted to see Pike about?"

"No."

"What brought you here so quickly? Anonymous phone call?"

Rawlins looked at me steadily for several seconds, without speaking. Then he said slowly, "You sound like you're already working for the man."

"Maybe. Maybe not. But I'd like to talk to him. How about it?"

He chewed his lip. "O.K. Make it fast."

"All right if I talk to Waverly alone?"

"Not a chance. Not even you, Shell. Right after this we're taking him downtown and booking him. He's it. You want to talk to him, O.K. But right here, with me."

"Fair enough. What did bring you guys here, Bill?"

"You tagged it. Phone call, no name, allegedly from a neighbor. But — get this — the call came from here. From twenty-two-seventeen Gable."

"The hell. If the call was anonymous, how come you know it was from this phone? Don't tell me you were able to trace — "

"No. We had a bit of luck there. After the call came in to the complaint board we checked the phone company. Routine, didn't expect anything. But the operator who handled the call was able to pin it down for us. The phone had been off the hook for two or three minutes. Then somebody — Waverly, undoubtedly — jiggled the hook, got the operator, and called us."

"Why Waverly undoubtedly?"

"Who else?"

"Do you really think he'd kill Pike and then call the law to come arrest him?"

"Knock it off, Shell. Why wouldn't he? Way it looks, he didn't plan to kill the guy. If it's Murder Two, after he cracked Pike he knew he could be placed here — by his office; even you could have pinned it down, as it turned out — so he dreamed up his cock-and-bull story and called us. Not a new story, by the way."

"True. So who clobbered him on the head?"

"It's a big lump, but nothing he couldn't have done all by himself, Shell. Probably figured that would make the picture look better."

"Motive?"

"That's the only thing we haven't got. We'll get it." He glanced at Waverly. "He's been stewing for a while now. Give me a minute with him, then come on over."

"Good enough."

I looked around some more. There was quite a bit of police activity, but that wasn't anything unusual, so I gave most of my attention to the room. The walls and ceiling were cream color, but the rest was done primarily in reds and purples, which is a combination that often blends very well. Not this time. This was the red of bloodshot eyes and the purple of bruises, and it looked like a drunk after a fight.

It struck me that the comparison was apt, since the joint looked as if there might have been a little knock-down and drag-out in it. A red end table lay on its side next to a purple divan, and a red and purple lamp — the guy had been *nuts* about red and purple — was a foot from the small table, its base cracked. An overstuffed chair, mate to the one Waverly was sitting in, was turned so it faced the wall. My deduction was that either somebody had banged into the thing and spun it about, or Pike had enjoyed looking at walls. Which, in this room, would have made a lot of sense.

Garish abstractions in gold frames were on two of the walls, and in addition to the small figure which had been used as the blunt instrument, several other idols or art objects were in various places about the room, including a six-inch-high figure that looked Indian, with its tongue stuck *way* out, and an oddly shaped receptacle closely resembling a ceramic chamber pot.

What kind of man, I wondered, could leave that orgiastic pink office and then come home to this?

More important, what kind of man was Gordon Waverly?

As far as reputation goes, he was cleaner than the gals who do those TV commercials in showers. The main reason for the almost automatic initial acceptance of his weekly, *Inside*, and the current respect for the accuracy and balance of its contents, was because of Waverly, himself. I guess he'd been in publishing most of his adult life. Writer, editor, publisher of a slick-paper short story magazine, then into book publishing. He was still the major stockholder in Waverly and Smith, Inc., the publishing company he'd founded fifteen or twenty years ago. In the fifty-odd years of his life he'd never been involved in a scandal. He was well liked, a member of numerous civic organizations, active in local politics — he'd even been asked to run for mayor, but declined — and of course he knew most of the "names" in Hollywood.

That did not mean, however, that he hadn't crushed Finley Pike's brainbox.

Rawlins turned, crooked a finger at me.

When I stopped in front of him, Gordon Waverly rose a bit unsteadily to his feet and stuck out his hand. I shook it as he said, "How do you do, Mr. Scott?" The voice was mellow, rich, and deep. "I had not anticipated such distressing circumstances when I asked you to meet me."

"Let's hope not." I glanced at Pike's body. "You kill him?"

"No."

That was all he said. Just the one bald word. He paused, then continued, "I phoned you regarding another matter. We'll forget that for now. But — did my receptionist give you the check?"

"Yes, she did."

He nodded. "Then I ask you to accept it as your retainer and endeavor to help me prove I did not kill Mr. Pike — and, of course, attempt to learn who the murderer truly is. Will you?"

No pleading, no big song and dance. I liked that. Assuming, of course, he hadn't pounded on Pike's head and was now sincerely pulling my leg out of its socket. I said, "I'm not certain what I'll do yet, Mr. Waverly."

"You'll have to give me your answer very soon. Before we leave. I'm to be charged with this crime."

"I know. What happened here? What's your story?"

He repeated exactly what Rawlins had already told me.

I said, "If you were standing by Pike's body and got clipped, how come you came to several feet away instead of next to Pike?"

"I was not standing, but kneeling. Why I came to my senses where I did, I have no idea. I remember nothing after the blow. . . . In fact, I do not now even recall the blow itself. Perhaps I staggered, crawled — I simply have no idea."

So far, so good. I said, "This little case on the floor near the body. You just glanced at it, and the papers? You weren't curious about it?"

"Of course not. It was simply an attaché case, apparently. It was lying open on the carpet with papers in it and spilling from it, as if it had been dropped. Mr. Pike was lying on the floor. I feared he had become ill, fainted, perhaps even suffered a heart attack or stroke. I assumed he had been carrying the case and dropped it as he fell. I also assumed, quite naturally I think, that he was merely unconscious. I had no idea. . . ." Waverly stopped for a moment, and his lips twitched slightly. "Then I saw his head."

Still pretty good. I said, "What about Natasha Antoinette?"

"I have nothing whatever to say about Natasha Antoinette."

Very good indeed. His eyes were still a bit dull from shock, but they were level and steady, fixed directly on my own.

Rawlins said, "What the hell's this about Natasha Antoinette?"

"Beats me," I told him.

He scowled slightly, but let it ride.

It did beat me; I didn't know what the hell it was about Natasha. But, besides that, I had just decided to go along with Mr. Waverly. Primarily because of his answer to my last question. Because he hadn't lied to me. He was holding out on me, obviously. But — at least in this one instance — he hadn't lied. And he could have, very easily.

He could have said, "Who?" or "I haven't the least notion what you're talking about, you idiot," or any number of things. But he'd simply said — and in front of Lieutenant Rawlins, at that — "I have nothing whatever to say about Natasha Antoinette."

Good for him. I cling to the old-fashioned notion, not only that Honesty Is the Best Policy but that it's the only one — the only one that works, anyhow. So I said, "O.K., Mr. Waverly. I'll accept your retainer. And I'll do what I can." I paused. "But Heaven help you if you killed him."

He smiled slowly. "I should think, rather, that it would be the other way around."

I grinned and suddenly realized that, ever since seeing him here in the room, with a body on the floor and blood on his head, I'd been trying not to like the guy. Without a great deal of success. I stopped trying and shook his hand again. "You're right," I said. "But I suppose I might as well nose about and dig up whatever I can."

"You might as well." He smiled again. "To the ultimate of your ability and, hopefully, clairvoyance."

"That's about what I had in mind."

Oh, we were getting along famously. We liked each other lots. We were about to kiss each other. Then Rawlins kind of spoiled our romance.

"You're actually going to bat for this joker?" he asked, as though entranced. Then he cleared his throat. "Um, pardon me. I mean, for Mr. Waverly. But — you're actually — "

"I actually am," I said, interrupting him. "I am now hired, obligated, retained, and thus shall exercise my brawn and wits — is it against the rules, Bill?"

"No . . ." He looked uncomfortable.

As I said, we were long-time friends. And a long-time friend does not like to see an old buddy stick his neck way out, like that idol's tongue, and lay it down on a block. Which, I gathered, he felt I was doing.

"There's a thing or two I didn't get around to mentioning," he went on after a pause. "For one, the joker — um, the individual — who killed Pike beat the daylights out of him first. There is ample evidence of that on the person of Mr. Pike, not to mention the appearance of the scene." He snorted gently through his nostrils. "Though you probably failed to notice the unmistakable evidence."

"I said, "A police captain once hinted I should not go around stepping on evidence and mashing it all up. So I haven't yet stepped on the late Mr. Pike. But I will, if it's accepted investigatory procedure. As for the physical evidence of a romp, I did dimly perceive it. Through a haze of red and purple gorgeousness. So?"

I just happened to catch Waverly's expression then. He looked amused.

This guy was either a very hard case or else a man of supreme poise and aplomb. He was, unquestionably, in a squeeze so tight it should have been pinching even his bladder, but he was nonetheless able to enjoy the spectacle of two imbeciles insulting each other. Either way, he did have that kind of stiff-upper-lip quality apparently born in certain Britishers, that "One more gin-and-tonic, lads, before we die for England" air. Of course, some of them, like mad dogs, went-out-in-the-noonday-sun, too; but Waverly seemed almost depressingly sane and level-headed.

I said again to Rawlins, "So?"

He shrugged. "Mr. Waverly?"

My client — by whom I had been hired, obligated, and retained, and for whom I would at least exercise my brawn — his expression not amused now but one of mild distaste, lifted his hands, palms down.

They were pretty well banged up, bruised, one knuckle split and with blood caked in the crack.

Almost as if he'd beaten the daylights out of somebody.

"Well," I said weakly. "How did *that* happen?"

Six

It was a rhetorical question, but Waverly answered it. "As I have already informed the lieutenant, I do not know how it happened. I do not know, but the explanation is transparent. I did not hit Mr. Pike. My hands were not like this when I was struck from behind. They were in this condition when I regained consciousness."

He left it there.

I said, "Look, Mr. Waverly, if you're trying to tell us this somebody-else killed Pike and then stomped on your hands, say, the lab in SID down at Central — *if* that's what happened — can almost come up with the size and price of the shoe he used for stomping. Those boys can split a gnat's eyelash so many ways it looks like a bug's wig — "

"Mr. Scott I am not trying to tell you anything except the facts as I know or understand them. I am quite aware of the seriousness of my position — "

"It's serious, all right."

"But I have seen no virtue in stressing the obvious. It is also obvious that I cannot prove I did *not* kill Mr. Pike, and therefore the preservation of my liberty and perhaps life requires demonstration that someone else did kill him. The truth is both sword and shield, and I can do no more than tell you the truth. Which is what I have done."

"O.K.," I said. An officer came over and showed Rawlins something on a paper in his hand. Waverly sat down again. I nosed around a bit, talked to a couple of officers I knew, checked the rest of the house, went to the bathroom. Purple can in there. That would just about constipate a man all by itself, I thought. Then I took a peek at Finley Pike, moments before they rolled him away.

He had been a man about five feet, six inches tall, maybe a hundred and twenty pounds, with a pale narrow face and a small brown mole alongside his nose. His eyes, now staring past limp, half-lowered lids, were blue. His face had obviously been pounded on, as if by someone tenderizing a steak, and his skull, of course, was very ugh. Aside from that he looked as if he'd been a nice, harmless, quiet guy. But you never know. On the fourth finger of his right hand he wore either a very vulgar rhinestone or a diamond ring of at least eight carats — it isn't so vulgar if it's a diamond. His suit was dark blue, apparently tailored, and the pale blue shirt was a custom job with small initials, FDP, monogrammed in darker blue over his left breast where a pocket would have been but wasn't. Neat, but not gaudy — except maybe for the diamond or rhinestone. I supposed he pulled down a pretty good chunk from his work for *Inside*. Whatever it was. I asked Rawlins about that.

Pike had been one of four vice presidents. Not too many, I guess, at least compared to some Hollywood firms which give a guy a pushbroom and a title, Vice President in Charge of Push-Brooms. Part of his job had been to oversee production of several of the most widely read and discussed departments and columns of the weekly, among them "Hits & Misses," a half-page showing the earnings and relative status of major films in release and television shows at or near the top or bottom of the public's favor, a kind of bestseller list of movies and TV productions. Also "Lifelines for the Lifelorn," bylined Amanda Dubonnet, one of those write-me-and-I'll-solve-your-problem-even-if-it's-unsolvable columns, which, despite the fact that I thought it seasoned with a bit too much gush and ick, was one of *Inside*'s most popular and most quoted features — possibly because it was, naturally, concerned primarily with the problems of people in show business. Pike had personally written "Goulash," a bright and witty potpourri of trade news, quotes, inside jokes, and showbiz miscellany.

I got next to Waverly for perhaps five seconds when nobody else was nearby and said, "Anything else you feel you should tell me?"

He shook his head.

"Not even about Natasha?"

"I've nothing to add. Not . . ." He hesitated. "Not now. I'd like to talk to you tomorrow. After I've . . . slept on this."

Rawlins walked up as I said, "I could come down to the jail if you — "

"No. There's no need."

I looked at Bill Rawlins, then back at Waverly. "If you want me to do a real job for you, it would be stupid to hold back any information that might help me."

He smiled slightly. "I am not stupid, Mr. Scott."

"That's what I figured. Well, I'm off." I turned to Rawlins. "See you outside for a minute, Bill?"

We went out front, and I said, "Check and see if you can turn up any kind of relationship between Waverly — or Pike — and Al Gant."

"Gant?" His eyebrows went up. "Why him?"

I told Bill about the near accident. "If it hadn't been Mooneyes at the wheel we might both have wound up scattered on somebody's lawn."

"Be damned," he said. "Ken mentioned you nearly got hit by a black sedan. But he couldn't see who was in it."

"Mooneyes, J. B. Kester, and two other mugs in back; I didn't make them. But, considering the company — "

"Yeah. It probably wasn't the mayor and the chief of police."

"Not quite."

"Think they were coming here?"

"Who knows? Wherever they were going, they were in a tizzy about getting there." I thought a moment. "Waverly's well known. But what do you know about Pike?"

"Nothing. I never even heard of him before tonight. We'll check his prints. Might help if he's got a record."

"Not likely — not if he was working for Waverly. But you never can tell. I'll drop in tomorrow, Bill, but if you come up with anything sticky on Waverly, give me a call, will you?"

He grinned. "You mean more than we've already got?"

I grinned back at him. "Hell, he couldn't have done it. He's my client."

"Very funny. Suppose he did."

"Then I'll break it off in him. I told him as much."

"Yeah. Thanks for the bit about Gant's boys."

I told him to take good care of Waverly, and left.

It seemed unlikely Mooneyes and Company would have been burning up the road to someplace just coincidentally near the spot where a murder had very recently occurred — they were usually there when it happened; but it seemed less likely their boss, Al Gant, could have had any connection with Waverly, or even Pike. True, he had a lot of "investments," in both legitimate and bastard enterprises — always through fronts, guys once or twice removed from him. He was careful; he'd done only one stretch in stir. But that one stretch had built in him a magnificent, a towering antipathy for the guy who, you might say, stirred him. You guessed it: me.

Al Gant. Born, Aldo Gianetti. Square, solid, built along the unsightly lines of a dump truck, with sloping shoulders and thick arms, and a belly like a beer barrel. Big square teeth with the beauty of little tombstones, all gray — except for one in front that was a kind of off-white. Man, he was a real brute; I figured he wore pants primarily to hide his tail.

Al and I went back quite a ways. The day we met — I'd been camping close to one of his hoods, a punk who'd muscled a friend of mine — Al was unwise enough to swing on me, and I knocked out one of his front tombstones. Now he had an off-white pivot tooth in front, and he didn't like pivot teeth at all, especially not in his own chops. Besides, it ruined the color scheme.

We met a few times after that, none of them real fun, and the last time — well, Al had killed a man named Vince, an operator on the fringe of the rackets, not quite in the Syndicate soup. Vince's widow hired me to tag his killer, and I did. I tagged Al Gant, pinned the job on him, and stuck him with it — lightly; he got unstuck. It was cold-blooded, premeditated homicide, Murder One; but he spent sixty G's for and through attorneys, copped a plea, drew one-to-ten in the state slammer, and did ten months. He'd been out for two and a half months now. Maybe he was getting old; maybe the prison chill was still in his bones, or maybe he was just biding his time. But he hadn't tried to kill me yet.

He would, though. You'd know that if you knew Al. And I knew Al.

One of the enterprises Al owned — though the owner on record was a guy named Pierce, who'd been financed by a man named Stone . . . and so on — was a restaurant and bar on Hollywood Boulevard called the Apache. Why it was called the Apache, since the hors d'oeuvres were garlic buds and the staple diet was starch, I've no idea. Maybe it had been called the Apache when Gant stole it, and he kept the name for sentimental reasons. Anyhow, he dawdled there much of the time, toying with a tasty dish of fettuccini and sauerkraut — or whatever they serve in those places. I'm not exactly up on Italian food.

At any rate, it had occurred to me that, *if* Al was somehow involved in Pike's murder, and if shortly after spotting his slobs in the vicinity of the murder scene I paid a call upon Al Gant himself, then even though I had nothing whatsoever to link Gant to Pike or Waverly, Gant would probably think I *did* have something.

Clever? Sure. A clever way to get a couple little pills in my head, the kind that cure headaches but do not dissolve gently in stomachs.

On the other hand, if Gant was just "biding his time," I preferred that the choice of time be mine, not his. So I drove down Hollywood Boulevard to the Apache.

Seven

Al Gant was at his usual table in the club's rear, close to the intersection of two walls, flanked by Mooneyes and another man I didn't recognize. He was eating something from a big plate, shoveling the gummy stuff into his mouth and talking to his two pals — with his mouth full, of course.

I stood at the end of the bar and watched him for a minute or two. An extension phone was on his table, and while I watched he took two calls, glowering. He looked as if something had spoiled his day for sure, and he hadn't even seen me yet. After he hung up for the second time I walked toward his table.

He was just about to fork a big gob of tastiness into his chops when he saw me. He stopped moving, mouth open and ready, eyes angled sideways at me. The gob on his fork balanced there briefly, then plopped onto his plate. His mouth moved, though. Either he thought he'd got the gob and was chewing, or else he was swearing. I kind of think he was swearing.

Actually, when I got close enough to hear him I discovered it was a little of both. He was swearing and chewing me out.

"Al," I said, "you should never eat when you're emotionally disturbed. According to nutritional science — "

"To hell with them bums. You got a nerve, comin' in here."

"Well, when I saw your two heavies out at Finley's I figured maybe it was time we had another chat." I looked at Mooneyes. "You and J. B. find any girls out there?"

He didn't answer me, but Gant said, "Finley's?"

"Finley Pike's."

"Who's he?"

"A guy who got killed tonight. Didn't you know?"
"How would I know?"
"That's what I was wondering."
"I don't even know who the jerk is."
"Well, maybe I can be wrong."
"The day you're right — that'll be the day."
"That's a peculiar thing for you to say, Al."

He scowled, remembering a day when I'd been right. The phone on his table rang, and, still scowling, he grabbed it. "Yeah, this is Gant," he said. While listening, his scowl went away, to be replaced by an expression that was perhaps as close to unbridled joy as that face could get. He even showed his big, square, gray teeth in a kind of smiling snarl. "Good," he said, "good, that's great. You'll be took care of — "

He broke it off. He didn't look at me, but he stopped talking suddenly and got up from the table, carrying the phone, a few feet of cord trailing behind him. Just out of earshot he talked for another minute or two, then came back to the table.

He was clearly happier when he sat down again. His day didn't appear to be ruined any longer, even with me here. Despite his improved disposition, Gant had nothing at all to tell me.

He didn't know Finley Pike; he didn't know Gordon Waverly; he didn't have any idea where J. B. Kester was; he didn't know the time of day, and even if he did he wouldn't give it to me within three hours. All of which was about what I expected.

So I prepared to leave and told Al I'd see him around, and he replied, "You can count on it, Scott."

The way he said it, I believed him.

Natasha Antoinette had an unlisted phone number, but I knew what it was. When I called, though, there was no answer.

Gordon Waverly's peculiar reticence about speaking of her had intrigued me, and I'd hoped a word or two from Natasha might provide a clue to his reticence. Or at least give me an idea what that original phone call had been about. If, of course, the sniffling woman on the phone had really been Natasha Antoinette.

Well, I'd try her again, later. In the meantime there was routine work to do. Partly by telephone, but mostly through visits to small smelly bars, apartment houses, and slightly down-at-the-heel hotels, I got in touch with certain men and women on my "list." They were the hangers-on, the small fry and occasionally fairly big fish, people both inside and outside of the rackets with a finger on the criminal pulse or at least ears sensitive to rumbles in the so-called underworld of the city — my sources of information, providers of leads and tips and rumors, the informants without which any investigator is a dead duck.

I was fishing for any connection between Al Gant and Gordon Waverly or Finley Pike, or for the knowledge, even a hint, of friction, trouble, bad blood between Waverly and Pike. Most of the people to whom I talked had never heard of Waverly or Pike. They knew who Al Gant was, though. And they didn't want any trouble with Al Gant.

But the word, if there was any to be had, would trickle to me. Some of the people on my list thought they owed me a favor, some wanted me to be a little in their debt, some would take money for information. A couple of them were, in a sense, on my payroll; I gave them money from time to time, and in return they slipped me information they thought I needed, or might need. One of those two, for example, a long-time burglar named Jim Gray, had — nearly a year before — passed on a bit of drunken conversation he'd overheard. An ex-con whose name I didn't even recognize, so the info went, was planning to blast me into two large halves with a shotgun. Thus forewarned I had been forearmed — with my .38 Colt Special and even greater than usual caution about venturing into spooky places — and, when Jim's information proved correct, I got off the first shot and the third, the second being the blast of a shotgun triggered convulsively, and wide of the mark, by the ex-con whose name I didn't even recognize, dying. Thus, thanks to Jim Gray, I was nearly a year older than I might otherwise have been. And — since as a result he was on my payroll for life — he had an interest in my living long.

Tonight I'd reached him by phone, and he was the only one of my informants to come up with anything even approaching helpful comment.

"Gordon Waverly?" he said. "Who's he?"

"Very big citizen," I told him. "Publisher of *Inside*."

"Hum. Yeah. I heard of it. Paper for the Hollywood wackos, ain't it?"

"Something like that. Trade paper, comes out weekly. This Finley Pike's one of the vice presidents. He got himself killed tonight."

"No kidding. Who done it?"

"Fuzz thinks it was Waverly. But maybe it wasn't. And I need to be sure."

"Yeah. Hum. Gant . . . Seems like I heard something about old Al, and . . ." He was silent for a while. "Something's rattling up there, but it's only another rattle, Scott. I'll nose around and get back to you. Tomorrow, maybe."

"Sooner the better."

"Well, tomorrow then, if I got something or don't. Say, I seen the cutest little TV and radio. It was in one box, dials on both sides, you could carry it around."

"Where'd you see it, Jim?"

He remembered where. He remembered the make, price, color, and amount of sales tax. I said, "Sounds like something you ought to have."

"It do, don't it? Talk to you tomorrow, Scott."

We hung up, and I made a mental note not to forget to send him the cutest little TV and radio, in one box.

In my apartment at the Spartan, with my shoes off and a mild bourbon-and-water handy on the cigarette-scarred coffee table, I called Homicide downtown. Rawlins was still in the squadroom and came to the phone.

"Hi," he said. "I suppose you've heard about the fuss out at Pikes?"

"Hear? I was there, remember?"

"No, I mean since then. About an hour ago."

"News to me. Fill me in."

"Ken and his partner were still there. Spotted a guy in the garage — right next to the house, you know?"

"Yeah. So?"

"He tried to lam out, made the mistake of trying to shoot his way out."

"Ken O.K.?"

"Flesh wound, nothing to worry about. But Kester's dead."

"Kester? J. B. Kester?"

"Uh-huh. I thought that would interest you."

"It sure as hell does. That sort of ties it together, doesn't it?"

"Ties something, not sure what."

"Kester was right alongside Mooneyes when they nearly thumped me. This makes it ten to one they must have been headed for Pike's house."

"Likely. But if so, Kester didn't have time to tell us why."

"Funny. His going there while police were still on the scene, I mean. What was he doing in the garage?"

"Don't know. Ken says they went all over the place, but it wasn't any help."

I told Rawlins about my brief dialogue with Al Gant and added, "Mooneyes was with him. But Kester wasn't, naturally." I thought a moment. "Just when did this happen? How long ago?"

"About an hour on the nose now."

That made it approximately the time I'd been talking to Gant at his table in the Apache. About the time he'd received that phone call, which seemed to have considerably brightened his day. It could, however, hardly have been news that one of his hired hands had been shot to death. At least, it didn't seem likely.

I told Rawlins about the call and Gant's reaction, but it didn't mean any more to him than it did to me. He told me there was nothing in the Records and Identification Division on either Waverly or Pike, and that they were waiting for the kickbacks from Sacramento and the FBI on both sets of prints. Waverly, after being booked, had apparently gone peacefully to sleep in his cell, without complaint or fuss — or further comment. My client was beginning to puzzle hell out of me.

We hung up; I finished my bourbon and went to bed. It was just midnight. Only three hours ago I'd been preparing to light the charcoal, have a Martini, and embark upon an evening which could — even though I now realized the chances had been about one in a thousand — have been glorious.

Instead I'd looked at a guy's spilled brains, and taken on a client who was now in the house of many slammers, and kind of halfway hinted to Al Gant that he ought to kill me.

I couldn't escape the feeling that, somewhere along the line, I might have made a little mistake.

Eight

The morning came up like mush, as usual, but black coffee opened my eyes and cleared my brain a bit. I called Natasha; no answer. But hell, the sun was up; she was a star; probably she'd left for work hours ago.

Over breakfast oatmeal I read the morning's *Herald-Standard*. Waverly was in the headlines, by occupation if not by name: PUBLISHER HELD IN MURDER CASE. Mild enough. His name was in the subhead: *Gordon Waverly, Publisher of* Inside, *Charged With Murder of Finley Pike.*

The story gave the facts clearly — and without undue emotion. But it was all covered quite thoroughly. It didn't look so good for Waverly. The shooting and death of J. B. Kester was given quite a bit of space since it was somewhat of a puzzler, and he'd had a long criminal record, which was included in the story. My name was mentioned as an investigator employed by the suspect. No mention was made of Al Gant, Mooneyes, or the other men who'd been in that speeding Imperial.

Toward the bottom of the front-page story some of Finley Pike's personal history was given, none of it scandalous. He'd been a newspaperman, had worked as a press agent for a few years, then edited a TV trade journal before going to work for Waverly.

After that there was a small shocker. "Mr. Pike, in addition to his other duties and his authorship of *Inside*'s popular feature 'Goulash,' personally wrote the column 'Lifelines For the Lifelorn' under the nom de plume of — *Please turn to Col. 4, Sec. A.*"

I turned to Col. 4, Section A. *"Amanda Dubonnet."*

There was more, but I paused to think, "Why, the little *monster*." So *he* was the character who'd written, with too much gush and ick, such un-deathless advice as that to a jilted orphan: ". . . So, dear child, see him no more — he's not for you! Cut him out of your bruised heart! And if ever you need sympathy or comfort again, write me. Ill always be here. Think of me, dear, as your mother. Sincerely, Amanda."

Some sincere mother, Finley. He wasn't here, either; he'd been wrong about that, too.

Oh, boy, I thought. I'll tell you the truth. I have never been able to understand the weird mental processes of people who write to the Amanda Dubonnets for advice on their physical, mental, spiritual, psychological, pathological, ontological, astrological, and hugely improbable problems. But, surely, even if they should perhaps better have written to an encyclopedia, they deserved something a bit more than a Finley Pike.

I read on to the end of the story, but there was nothing else of equal fascination. Yes, fascination — in the Amanda bit there'd been a clue. Maybe that jilted orphan — or one of her brothers or sisters — had killed Finley-Amanda. If so, in a different world, it might have been adjudged justifiable homicide. And maybe I was reaching, too; maybe Gordon Waverly had in truth, and unjustifiably, committed homicide upon Finley's head.

With that slightly sour thought fermenting inside my own head, I went to work.

I didn't go straight down to see Waverly. Under the circumstances I wanted to know a bit more about what was going on before I talked to my client again. I wanted to be a bit more sure, that is, that he was going to remain my client.

Natasha Antoinette was emoting in Jeremy Slade's latest doozy, *Return of the Ghost of the Creeping Goo,* and I finagled the location where shooting was going on this day. It was little more than ten miles out in the boondocks, so I aimed the Cad that way and went.

A dirt road led off the highway, and when I was a mile down it I could see the activity on my right, where morning sunlight glanced from the chrome and metal of parked cars, and beyond them cameras and booms and lights and reflectors. People moved about in colorful costumes, many of the garments flesh-colored.

The plume of dust behind the Cad would have signaled my arrival even if I'd been trying to sneak up on the moviemakers, which I wasn't. Consequently, when I parked among the other cars a short and rotund fellow with a look of mild exasperation on his round face was waiting for me.

"We're shooting a picture here, you know," he said a bit stiffly.

"I do know," I replied pleasantly. "That's why I'm here. I'd like to talk to — "

"You can't talk to anybody, mac. These people are in the middle of a scene right — "

"I know," I said less pleasantly. "But not every little instant. I'd merely like a word or two with Natasha Antoinette, in a moment of relative idleness." I climbed out of the Cad and looked down at him. "All right?"

"Well, it's not up to me, mac. But — "

"I promise not to wave at the camera."

"Look, mac — "

"*Quit calling me mac!* Please?"

He went back a step. "Maybe . . . we better ask somebody. Slade or somebody."

"A fine idea."

He turned and walked toward the people and equipment. I followed him. Actually, the performers weren't in the middle of a scene at the moment. I recognized Jeremy Slade, his back to me, talking to the picture's director, who was seated in a canvas chair. Several yards to their right were forty or fifty people, some of them quite misshapen — half in and half out of monster costumes — but some of them very nicely shapen indeed. They were the toothsome starlets found in all Jeremy Slade productions, and they, too, appeared to be half out of their costumes. What I'd thought flesh-colored outfits were in many cases expanses of flesh-colored starlet.

One of the most outstanding expanses was a big Amazonian blast of a babe, busty, butty, ungirdled, and uninhibited, who had appeared in both of the first two *Goo* movies and who possessed the improbable name of Vivyan Virgin. Hell, let's be honest; it wasn't merely improbable, it was a downright lie. Vivyan was the gal responsible for the expensive delay in Slade's last picture. I wasn't sure just what had been wrong with her. All I'd heard was that she'd been "ill," and in Hollywood that can mean anything from terminal laryngitis to a hangover.

The guy who'd met me at the parking lot had walked over toward Slade, and I didn't have a keeper at the moment. So when I spotted

Natasha Antoinette sitting a couple yards from Vivyan Virgin I waved and started walking toward her. There wasn't any filming going on, and I didn't think anybody would have a fit if I moved around just a little. Natasha waggled her hand in reply and smiled.

She and another girl were seated in canvas-backed chairs under a beach umbrella. Nat was a tall, black-haired, sensationally-shaped tomato wearing a kind of Grecian-Venusian white gown cut in a low loop that exposed just enough of her famous chest to get by the censors if she didn't lean over at all. The gown was ankle-length, but was pulled up now over her knees, exposing the slim but shapely brown legs.

I stopped next to her and said, "Hi, Nat."

"Hello, Shell." The voice was deep, smooth, velvety. "I didn't expect to see you out here."

"Didn't expect to be here."

"Welcome. Stick around for my dance." She smiled and blinked the big black eyes at me.

Those eyes — they were fantastic, compelling, almost hypnotic — like black diamonds on fire, satanic, slanted, smoldering. They were eyes that could cut ten feet through a London fog, eyes to cook a man's gizzard, eyes to boil blood with.

My blood was getting ready to sizzle my gizzard when Natasha slanted her glance away from me to the girl sitting with her under the umbrella. "This big lump is Shell Scott, Cherry," she said. "Shell, Cherry Dayne."

"How do you do?" I said.

"Hello, Mr. Scott."

"Shell, please. Pretend we're old friends."

"I'd love to."

And I'd love for her to love to, I thought. This one had everything Natasha had, and in approximately the same percentages, since she was two or three inches shorter. And, of course, lighter in color, since in the film she apparently played the part of one of the lesser Venusians. She was wearing a gown like Natasha's, but instead of being ankle length it extended down only to her knees. When she was standing up, that is. Sitting down, it didn't extend nearly that far. Just far enough, I thought.

And if Natasha's eyes seemed filled with something like light from outside space, this Cherry's sparkled with the electricity that makes the world go around. They were bright and clear and a vivid blue, the kind of eyes you'd expect on the devil if the devil were incandescently female, and friendly.

But I couldn't just stand there looking from eyeball to eyeball, no matter how exciting it was. I'd come here for a purpose. It had occurred to me, however, that Natasha might not want to discuss last night in front of a third party, so I said, "Nat, as long as you're not busy at the moment, could I have a word with you alo — "

That was as far as I got.

A hand squeezed my left bicep like a steel octopus, and I was yanked around much more vigorously than I like to be yanked around. In fact, I do not like guys laying large hands on me even in gay good fellowship.

So I wasn't smiling when I got my feet planted again and stared at the guy facing me. It was Jeremy Slade.

I said, "Don't do that again."

Before the words were out of my mouth he growled, "What the hell do you think you're doing here?"

I chewed on my teeth for a few seconds, took a deep breath, and calmed down. After all, it was his picture. If he wanted to kick me the hell off the premises, or chew me out, I couldn't very well complain.

So I said, "Just saying hello to an old friend." I glanced at Cherry and added, "And a new one." She smiled dazzlingly.

Slade reached for my arm again and said, "Come on over here."

I raised a hand and blocked his clutching fingers. "Uh-uh. Don't grab." I tried to smile. "Just lead the way."

He grunted, then turned and walked off to a cleared area where nobody else was standing, then turned to face me.

Slade was about five-ten and two hundred pounds, solid and blocky, his shoulders broad and his midsection lean. He looked fit and healthy, but his face was a sculptured scowl. He usually wore the expression of an astronaut going up in a space capsule against his will, sort of squashed and belligerently angular, and a bit tortured. One guess was that he was a size forty man wearing size thirty shorts; at least, his features seemed stamped with the marks of pinching, strangulation, and a dull ache.

That, if true, might have explained his voice, as well, for it came out of a thick chest and muscled neck in an incongruously high-pitched toot or tweet. Even from a tall, pale, weedy cat the voice would have seemed too thin, but fluting from Slade's thick lips it was the sound of a dedicated birder trying to communicate with his feathered friends.

I told him who I was, and that I wanted a word with Natasha; and now he tweeted, "What do you want to talk to her about?"

"Nothing important, probably, Mr. Slade. Just trying to corroborate some information given me by a client."

"Who's the client?"

"I'd rather not say."

"You'd rather not say."

He scowled at me as if suddenly suffering about two more G's of boost. And when Slade scowled on purpose he did an extremely good job of it. He had eyebrows bigger and bushier and more tangled than some toupees. A flea could have lived and died in there without ever seeing daylight. Actually, they were more like one wide brow, since the two of them grew together in the middle, as if his nose had started out as hair and then grown longer and harder, like the horn of a rhinoceros.

Finally he lifted the brow up, peeled his lips apart, squeezed them back down over his teeth. "You'd rather not say. Well, I guess that's your business."

"Yes, sir."

He was silent for a few moments. "Can't it wait?"

"Not very long."

"Well, O.K., you can talk to her — but not till we've shot the dance scene."

"When will that be?"

"Some time this morning. Depends on whether these idiots remember their lines or not. Once in a while they do. Might be an hour. If we're all lucky."

He didn't strike me as a man who felt lucky; and bad luck did seem to pursue him. I've mentioned the delay on his previous film, when the second female lead was out of circulation for several days. And then, shortly after shooting had started on this picture, it was very nearly delayed by Slade's being out of circulation himself. This time shooting had begun on Wednesday, April first — appropriately, I thought, on April Fool's Day — and on the following Saturday night, with only three days of the shooting schedule marked off, Slade had missed a curve on his way home and gone down a hundred feet or so into a rocky canyon. At least, his brand-new black Cadillac had gone down; Slade himself had jumped from the car — according to the newspaper story I had read — and wound up with a bruised head, plus miscellaneous bangs and scrapes. I understood he'd had an arm in a sling for a few days, but he was still lucky to be shooting his third *Goo* epic, now — if you call that lucky.

I said, "All right if I wait?"

He shrugged. "Stick around if you want to. Just stay the hell away from Natasha till she's done her scene." He paused. "She's temperamental as hell, and I don't want you — or anybody else — stirring her up till she's done. If that happened, I could get kind of temperamental myself."

He made it sound as if there'd be eclipses of the sun and moon if Natasha got stirred up. Hell, she was maybe a little wild — and wild-eyed — but she was not the fuse of total destruction.

However, I said, "Fair enough. Thanks, Mr. Slade."

He grunted. I strolled away, letting an eye rove over the activity. It was an interesting rove. An hour later I'd watched one scene shot twice, talked to an old friend named Ed Howell, and spent a few more minutes with lovely Cherry Dayne. She told me she had to run away from some oysters and get rescued by Ed, then she'd be finished for the day.

The crew was ready for that scene now, and I watched, very attentively, as Cherry ran, in fetching deshabille and simulated panic, from the monsters clacking behind her. . . .

Nine

Natasha's Dance.

Finally.

If it was any better than Cherry's running, I figured it should be the high point of the movie. Maybe even the high point of my day.

Natasha seemed to have recovered completely from her recent fainting spell, or whatever it had been. Now she stood in the midst of a whole lot of hairy people, the hairiest of whom was Gruzakk.

The other, I understood, were his rebellious white soldiers, who had captured the black Venusian queen and brought her to their chief; they looked very disgruntled, as if thinking they would rather have kept her. I didn't blame them. With the sunlight behind her pouring through the filmy veiling she wore instead of earth clothing, she nonetheless looked pretty earthy. The warm light limned the outlines of her long, sensationally curved body like the dark cloud's silver lining, and she stood with her head thrown back, black hair crumpled on one shoulder.

Gruzakk, dressed in some kind of hairy animal skin — not his own — sat on a mound of earth covered with more animal skins, his back to me. One hairy arm rested on his hairy thigh, and from his hand a gleaming sword slanted downward to the ground before his feet. Of course, three cameras were turning, there were men standing barely out of camera range holding foil-covered reflectors and a mike boom, Phrye was riding a camera boom, and about fifty other people were massed in the area watching, but if I concentrated hard I could almost believe it was a real movie.

Gruzakk raised his sword and gave it a casual flick through the air. That was the signal. Natasha had to come on strong or Gruzakk would say "Fooey! Off with her head." I hadn't seen the script so I couldn't be sure that was the actual dialogue, but I'd have laid eight to five it wasn't far off the mark.

Well, she came on strong.

She started slowly, and there was nothing weak even about that part, but then she moved that gorgeous torso in a fluid wiggle, and a willowy shake, and then a sort of figure eight, and then maybe a nine, and finally what I guess was about a sixty. Anyway, she was going like sixty, and not like a gal all alone out there, but as if she were with company she liked a *lot*.

Well, there's only so much a woman can do in a dance, and there's only so much you can say about a woman dancing. But I'll say this: If Natasha had done that dance in Pasadena she'd have defrosted refrigerators in Glendale. Or, rather, vice-versa — you can't dance like that in Pasadena.

When the sequence ended she was standing with her back to the cliff, below her the Lake of Fire — lighted again, of course — sun hugging her wonderful body. A veil dropped. And I figured she'd been wearing only two veils to begin with. A camera was dollying in for a close-up — though without that other veil I figured this shot might wind up on the cutting room floor or in the producer's private library — and Natasha stood quite still with her arms thrown wide, head back, breasts thrusting forward deliciously. Toward Gruzakk.

He was leaning forward, as if about to fall onto the butt of his sword, as if about to make up unrehearsed dialogue — not "Fooey! Off with her head!" but rather "Off with her head? Fooey!" Or something equally appropriate.

I was, for that brief moment, eyeing Gruzakk.

So I missed it.

I did hear the scream.

It wasn't much of a scream. More like a loud, high-pitched sigh. I didn't even know at first that it had come from Natasha.

But when I flicked my eyes toward her again she was falling.

She just dropped back over the cliff's edge and out of sight, arms collapsing as she fell.

It was so quiet in those next few seconds that I heard — we could all hear — the splash as she hit the flame-covered water forty feet below.

It might have been in the script. Might have — but I didn't think so. She hadn't fallen gracefully backward; she'd fallen awkwardly, turning, arms bending in, elbows akimbo. If it *was* in the script, the scene was about to be ruined — because I was about to ruin it. As I ran forward I peeled off my coat, slapped my gun from its holster, and dropped it and the coat halfway to the cliff's edge.

At the edge I slid to a stop. I couldn't see Natasha. But below me in the smoky red flames boiling over the lake's surface was one spot free of fire, an irregular ring where the water still churned. As I watched, the ring of fire closed still more.

I picked a spot two or three yards from that closing ring, sucked my lungs full of air, and jumped.

I could feel the heat on my hands and face as I went down. My shoes hit the water with a slap, and before my head plunged beneath the surface I was sweeping my hands down and to the sides, trying to slow my descent.

I never did hit bottom. Enough sunlight came through the oil and flame on the water's surface to provide dim illumination when I opened my eyes; it mingled with the flickering redness of the burning oil and turned the blurred scene into something out of a watery hell, a red-tinged darkness that pulsed and billowed, moved like something huge and alive around me.

And in that pulsing movement I saw her, saw Natasha. She was below me, to my left, dim and dark, not yet on the lake's bottom. One arm floated alongside her, bent gracefully at wrist and elbow; the other hung almost straight down beneath her. She was turning slowly in the water, turning toward me. Her mouth was open.

I kicked hard, swept my hands through the water, moved next to her. I could barely see them, but her eyes were slitted, the lids not quite closed. My heart was starting to pound, lungs straining for air. I got an arm around her, beneath her breasts, and started swimming, staying under the water.

I had to breathe. As I went up to the lake's surface I swept my free hand back and forth above me, then, when my head broke through I swung my arm in a circle, splashing the burning oil and water from me. I could feel the heat. The wetness of my face kept it from burning the skin, but I could feel it in my lungs as I filled them with gulps of air. Sweeping my arm away from me and then stroking with it, I pulled Natasha the few feet remaining to the lake's shore. When my feet touched the soft bottom I picked her up and stumbled onto dry ground. She hung very heavy in my arms, limp, her head dangling.

Even before I placed her on the ground I saw the blood.

Ten

The blood welled from a small hole beneath Natasha's left breast.

When I took my left hand from her back it was smeared with sticky redness. I turned her over gently, though there was really no need for gentleness. The hole in her back was an inch or two lower and several times as large as the one beneath her breast. The exit wound always is much larger.

She'd been shot. And, of course, she was already dead.

Sweet, warm Natasha. Her eyes were still slitted, and I pressed the lids down. Over those hot black-velvet eyes — eyes that had been hot, had been glittering, burning, and a little brazen, eyes like none other; just parts of her dead flesh now.

As I stood up, Slade, Ed Howell, Phrye, and another man were coming down a path slashed in the side of the cliff. Dozens of other men and women were grouped above them looking down at us. Ed was the first to reach me. He went right by and dropped to his knees by Natasha. Then Slade arrived, panting from the climb down.

"What the hell happened?" he half-yelled. The too-high voice seemed as thin and taut as the voice of a woman about to have hysterics.

"She's dead," I said.

"Dead? *Dead?*"

"That's right. Somebody shot her."

"Shot? You're a damned . . ." His voice trailed off. He was looking down at Natasha. "Oh, my God," he said.

Ed held one of Natasha's hands in both of his own. His eyes were wide, staring, and his lips looked dry. Walter Phrye was with us now, babbling something at me. But I wasn't listening.

I sprinted to the path in the cliff, ran up it as fast as I could. It was steep, and my lungs hurt a little when I got to the top.

I looked at the spot where Natasha had been standing — the men and women were grouped there now, men in animal skins, women in gauzy stuff and in normal clothing, even the damned oysters and beetles — then I turned my head left, toward the spot from which the shot must have come.

The bullet had been traveling downward, had sliced through her ribs and come out lower, near her spine. There were two places, two hills or mounds of earth where the rifleman — it must have been a rifle — would have been. He wouldn't be there now.

Far to my left, a mile away on the dirt road I'd come down an hour or more ago, a plume of dust rose into the air just as dust had billowed behind my Cad earlier. I couldn't tell what make or model the car was, not even whether it was a coupe or sedan.

The crowd at the cliff's edge moved toward me, surging this way as if one of them had moved and the others were following automatically. I trotted to them. As I reached the group and turned, movement on my left caught my eye. Somebody running this way from the parking lot — Cherry. I could recognize her now, even though she was dressed in street clothes. That was right, she'd gone over there to change.

There was a babble of voices. Closest to me was Dale Bannon, an ace cameraman fallen — at least temporarily — to this low estate, actually *operating* a camera for Slade. I'd known him for a long time. So I talked to him, while the rest listened. I told him what had happened, that Natasha had been shot, that she was dead, and asked if he — or anybody else — had heard anything, seen anything, that might help pin down what had happened.

They hadn't. But, neither had I. I hadn't even heard the shot. There must have been some kind of silencer on the rifle. And that didn't indicate an amateur killer.

A woman — it was big, abundantly curved Vivyan — said in a small voice, "She's dead? Did you say she's dead?"

"Yes. Get it through your heads, all of you, she was murdered. Not just dead — murdered. So if you can remember — "

I didn't finish it. Cherry had run up while I was speaking and, gasping for breath, she said, "What? Murdered? Who — "

Somebody in the crowd wailed, "Natasha, somebody *shot* her."

Cherry's eyes were wide. "He shot her? Is that what he did? Why, I — "

"Shut up."

I was too slow. Just a half-second too slow.

She blurted it out. ". . . Saw him, I *saw* him. I didn't know he'd shot somebody, but I saw him running to the parking lot. He got into a — "

"Shut up, Cherry!"

" — Car and went. . . . What?" She turned the big blue eyes on me, not comprehending.

Hell, it was too late anyway. But I said, "Skip that for the moment, Cherry. No need to tell it twice — we have to call the police. There's a radio-telephone in my Cad. Come on with me while I call the cops, O.K.?"

She was looking around at the others, then past the cliff's edge to the four men and still body below. She blinked at me, and I thought — now — she looked a little frightened. "All right, Shell," she said, her voice subdued.

We left the others, headed back toward the parking lot. On the way I said to her, "O.K., you saw the guy — or at least a guy. Tell me what you can about him, Cherry."

Instead of answering directly she said, "I guess I shouldn't have yelled all that — in front of everybody. That's what bothered you, wasn't it?"

"It's probably all right," I said. But then I decided I might as well give the whole thing to her, and went on, "But you'll have to consider the possibilities, Cherry. If you saw the guy who killed Natasha, and he learns who you are and that you can identify him, he might . . . well, frankly, he might try to kill you."

She paled a little, but said, "I finally thought of that. A little late."

"Did you get a good look at the guy? And how about you, did he see you?"

"Yes, he saw me. You know I was changing in my car, instead of going back to the studio with the rest later. I'd just gotten out of my car when I saw this man. He was running toward the parking lot."

"From where?"

We were almost at the parked cars now, and she pointed to one of the two hills I'd been looking at earlier. "There, I guess. He was about halfway between there and me. I was right alongside my car." She pointed to a pale blue Corvette Sting Ray near us. "He didn't see me at first," she continued. "He was carrying — it looked like a little suitcase."

"Uh-huh. Must have had the rifle broken down in it."

"Anyway, he ran to a car, but saw me just before he reached it."

"Where was the car? And what kind was it?"

"I don't know what kind, just a big dark sedan. But it was right there." She pointed to a now-empty space between a Ford and a Chrysler.

"Probably figured a single car all by itself would be too conspicuous," I said. "Parking right in the lot wasn't a bad idea at that. What did he do when he saw you?"

"Stopped and stared at me. That's all. Then jumped into his car and drove off very fast. It puzzled me a little, but I didn't know any . . . he'd shot somebody, or anything."

"No way you could have, Cherry. You didn't hear a shot even from out here?"

She shook her head.

"O.K., what did the man look like?"

We were at my Cadillac, so I climbed in and reached under the dashboard for the phone, called the police while she talked.

"I hardly remember now. I didn't know I'd have to remember."

"As near as you can get it."

"He was tall. Thin, I think. Yes, he was thin, narrow face, too. That's . . . about all."

"How old was he?"

"Oh, older than you. Maybe forty, or forty-five."

"Dark hair, light, bald? Mustache? Anything unusual?"

She shook her head again.

"Clothes? Unusual coat or hat or anything?"

"No . . . he wasn't wearing a hat. And he wasn't bald, so he had hair — I can't remember whether it was dark, or anything. I'm sorry."

"No reason to be sorry. But if you think of anything else, any time, let me know right away." I hoped she did think of something else. So far it was a tall thin guy with hair.

I completed the call, informed the answering officer about what had happened, and gave the location. As I hung up, I said to Cherry,

"Incidentally, if you should want to phone me, call this number." I scribbled it on a piece of paper.

She took it and said, "Aren't you in the book?"

"Yeah, one of the phones is. But there's another in the bedroom, unlisted."

She smiled slightly. "In the bedroom?"

"It's a sort of special phone.... I mean, most of the people who have that number are guys who might call me any time of day or night. Even when I'm in the bedroom. Asleep in the bedroom. With information, I mean." I wondered why I got so sort of flustered when Cherry mentioned bedrooms. "Call me with information, I mean," I went on. "Sometimes I just let the front-room phone ring. But I answer the bedroom phone very rapidly. See?"

She smiled, and I said, "Are you going to stick around? Of course, you'll have to stay at least till the police get here."

Her smile went away. "Well, I do want to talk to Ed. He's probably shaken up by this. He liked Nat a lot, you know."

"Yeah, that's right. What happened to them? They had quite a thing going for a while, I thought. Then, zoop, it cooled."

She shrugged. "What happens to anybody? I don't know."

In a minute she walked back toward the movie company, and I walked to the hill she'd indicated. I approached its crest from the opposite side and did not stomp around all over the place, but it wasn't difficult to find the spot where the killer had been. Not only were there marks in the soft earth, in a kind of depression at the hill's top, but I spotted five cigarette butts. Interestingly, each one was smoked clear down to the filter. Even if I'd gone closer, or picked them up, I wouldn't have been able to make out the brand. But I didn't go closer.

A private detective is a private citizen, and police officers — as I'd told Rawlins, who already knew it, last night — take an exceedingly dim view of private citizens who barge about fiddling with evidence.

So I just stood a few feet off and looked down at the people near the cliff. It had been a damned good, or lucky, shot. But he'd probably had a powerful rifle with which he was thoroughly familiar, and telescopic sights. Too, it was a still day, no wind to worry about.

Anyway he'd killed her. Natasha was dead.

So, finally, I asked myself: Who? Who had wanted her dead?

And a somewhat disturbing thought started nagging me. Probably Natasha couldn't have told me much, but at least she could have said whether or not she'd been with Waverly last night. And, if she had been, she might have been able to tell me what that original call was all about. Mainly I'd hoped she could corroborate the story my client had given me.

She couldn't corroborate it now.

And did that leave Waverly smelling like a rose, or something else? Somehow, at least for the moment, he didn't smell so sweet to me.

Eleven

It was another forty-five minutes before I got away from there. The police arrived, I told them what I knew — and what Cherry had said in front of about fifty other people — and told the investigating officers who I was and where they could reach me.

Then I drove back to town.

I had to stop at my apartment — to wash off the dirt and oil, change clothes, and clean my gun, which had bounced in the dirt a bit before I got back to it — so while there I used the phone to check again with the men and women I'd called last night.

Jim Gray wasn't at his number but he'd left word where I could find him and that he wanted to see me; from the rest, nothing.

Gray was at a small bar on Brea a couple of blocks from Sunset. I found him there on a stool drinking beer, caught his eye, and jerked my head. He met me outside and climbed into the Cad.

I drove down Brea and said, "Got anything for me, Jim?"

"Maybe a little. You asked about this Pike or Waverly and Gant or his boys. Well, I didn't hear nothing about this Pike — except he's dead." He grinned. "You were sure right about that, huh?"

"Yeah."

Jim Gray had a knobby, lined face and thin gray hair, but a young smile. His two front teeth were crooked and poked forward in the middle of his mouth like the bow of a small canoe, and they gave his smile an almost impish appearance. He wasn't impish.

"How about Waverly?"

"He and Gant must be pretty thick. You told me about him publishing that paper *Inside* — you didn't know the rest of it, huh?"

"Come on, Jim, what rest of it? I ordered that damn TV set for you. It'll be delivered this afternoon."

"Hey, man, that's great — but you didn't have to do that. Well, Waverly must know Gant pretty good. Al put up the money so's he could start his little paper."

"Gant did? *He* put up the cash to start *Insider*?"

"Yeah, you got it."

"You sure, Jim? It could be pretty important."

"Sure I'm sure. I ever give you a bum steer?"

He hadn't, at that; and he'd given me some very good ones. "Any details?"

"Well, you know Gant, he don't sign no papers or nothing like that. Way I get it, Scott, he give the money to an old beast name of Madelyn Willow — used to be in the movies, I guess — and she put up the dough. That's all I could scrounge, but it looks to me like Waverly must've had some idea where the money really come from."

"Yeah, You'd think so." There was another intriguing angle to what he'd told me. Madelyn Willow was, indeed, a former actress. She was the ex-actress who owned the acreage on which Slade's current film was being shot. Maybe it didn't mean anything. For that matter, maybe none of Jim's info meant anything — yet.

That was all Jim had for me, so I dropped him off a couple of blocks from the bar where I'd found him. As he got out of the Cad I said, "You see anything else that enamored you while window-shopping?"

"Enam . . . What?"

"Anything else you thought was cute."

"Hum. Oh, no. But If I pick up any more info I'll sure let you know."

"Do that, Jim."

He strolled down the street.

And I decided it was time — now — for me to call upon Gordon Waverly.

I phoned the Police Building and learned that my client was no longer in jail. Under California law, when a man is charged with an offense punishable with death, he can't be admitted to bail "when the proof of his guilt is evident or the presumption thereof great"; nonetheless he'd been sprung.

Part of the reason, I gathered, was that the suspect was Gordon Waverly. But more, the police had — as yet — not even a smell of possible motive. Means and opportunity, of course, but not the third leg of the prosecutor's tripod. And certainly there was no evidence he'd been lying in wait, or that the murder had been "willful, deliberate, and premeditated." Also the kickbacks from the FBI and Sacramento had been blank on both Waverly and Pike.

Consequently, Waverly was charged with murder in the second degree — which is bailable. And he was out. In fact, he and his attorneys had left the Police Building only minutes before my call.

I stayed on the phone long enough to learn that the Crime Lab had worked over the ivory idol and found not only quite a bit of Finley Pike on it but also traces of another blood type, which was the same type as Gordon Waverly's. It could have come from Waverly's pounding on Pike with his fists and then using the idol itself on Pike, or — the view I argued — from his hands being pounded and bloodied by somebody else, the real killer, swinging the idol after using it on Pike. Neither the police nor I won that argument.

So I headed for an argument with Gordon Waverly.

I parked next to the *Inside* building, went in through the sighing glass doors, and stopped before the bosomy blonde receptionist. She made an "O" of her mouth and blinked, big-eyed, at me.

"Hi," I said. "Is Mr. Waverly here yet?"

"He just came in. Just this minute, practically."

"Fine, I'd like to see him."

"He went right by me. Like last night."

"Shouting?"

"Ha-ha," she laughed. "Goodness, no. He didn't say a word. And I thought surely he would. After all that's happened. After . . . all."

Oh, she was bubbling with curiosity, overflowing with unasked questions. Unasked, but about to be asked any instant.

"Well, I'd like to see him," I said.

"Yes. I'll buzz him. I guess you found him last night, didn't you?"

"Yeah. And I'd like to find him again, if it's all right. I'd like to see him. You know, today. In fact, as soon as possible."

She got a hurt look. First Waverly wouldn't talk to her, and now I wouldn't talk to her. Men were against her. Ha, if only she knew. I kind of think she did know. Especially in that scoopy blouse, with its wowy neckline.

She waited, but I outwaited her. Finally she fiddled with the intercom and said, "Mr. Waverly, Mr. Shell Scott is here to see you." She still remembered my name, but she didn't coo it this time. Of course, it's a little hard to coo it.

I heard Waverly's voice, flattened by the intercom. "Splendid. Send him right in, Miss Prinz."

Maybe, I thought, it wasn't going to be so splendid. But following Miss Prinz' directions I went to the hallway, left two doors, and into Gordon Waverly's office.

It was a big room and — I was grateful to note — not pink. Pale beige paneled walls, burnt-orange carpet, darker beige divan and chairs. Neat and not too gaudy. Waverly's desk was a big gray-brown job made of something like pecky cypress or cedar, behind it an oversized leather chair studded with brass buttons along the seams. And in the chair, Gordon Waverly.

He was wearing the same clothes he'd had on last night, but he looked spruce and gay, as if he were about to leave for a party. His lean, tanned face had been recently shaved, his tie was neatly knotted, and he looked rested. A small white bandage marred the smoothness of his straight gray hair. He was smiling as I entered. I wondered if he'd heard about the murder of Natasha Antoinette.

"I see you got sprung from jail," I said.

"Yes." He nodded. "I had much to think about, and finally phoned my attorneys. I've decided I should tell you all I know about the events of last night."

"It's about time. Or rather, it's a little late."

He pushed his eyebrows up, pulled them down. "What does that mean?"

"It means whatever you've got to say had better be damned good."

He did the bit with his eyebrows again, but remained silent. So I said, "Maybe I'd better tell you just how good. Let's start at the beginning, with our initial talk on the phone — and I still don't know what that was about. A woman, allegedly Natasha Antoinette — "

"Allegedly? Mr. Scott, I assure you — "

I went right on, " — Merely said hello, and then reported that you wanted to talk to me. At your request I came to your office, but you'd left. I found you at Finley Pike's. Curiously, as I arrived there a carful of hoodlums was also arriving, precipitously. They belonged to a mobster, blackmailer, slob, and killer named Al Gant. Later, after you'd been hauled to the can, the police shot and killed a heavy man named J. B. Kester outside the garage at the home of Finley Pike. Kester just happened to be one of the men in that carful of Gant's hoodlums. I've today learned that the same Al Gant put up the money which started, or at least helped to start, *Inside*."

His jaw had been slowly drooping, indelicately, which wasn't like Gordon Waverly at all — unless that's the impression he desired to convey. Now his jaw dropped even farther open, and he started to speak but thought better of it.

I finished it up. "I happen to know Natasha Antoinette, and tried to get in touch with her — my reason being, to tell you the truth, to find out if she really was with you last night, and if she could explain what the original fuss was about. With you in the can I didn't think there was any great rush, but I was wrong. I'd have worked a lot faster, and harder, if I'd had any idea she was going to be killed."

He paled. Visibly. I didn't know how he could have faked that. But there might have been a number of reasons for his apparent shock.

He said something, finally, but his voice was so low I couldn't hear the words. "What?" I asked him.

He swallowed and repeated, "Killed? Did you say killed?"

"The more accurate word would be murdered."

He didn't speak. I waited. He closed his eyes, moistened his lips, then blinked and looked at me. "When did this happen, Mr. Scott?"

"This morning. About ten A.M., maybe a little after. I was a bit too busy to note the exact time."

He said quite softly, "I'm afraid I should have told you a good deal more last night."

"No kidding."

He stared past me, not speaking.

"That's all I've got to say," I told him. "For now. But it leaves a lot of questions unanswered — by you. And if you can answer them all, you're damned good."

"I can't." His sharp-boned face looked a little gray. "I can't," he said again. "Oh, my actions — " he waved a hand in a fluttering gesture — "those I can explain. But the rest . . ." He licked his lips again. "How was Miss Antoinette killed?"

"She was shot. By someone using a rifle. While before the cameras in Jeremy Slade's current production. Isn't it time you came up with some answers instead of questions?"

He straightened in his chair and looked at me, and his jaw firmed a bit. He said levelly, "Are you eager to retire from my employ, Mr. Scott?"

He sounded a little hardboiled. Either he figured, as he'd once indicated, that an attack was the best defense, or there was more than a little backbone in his back.

"I laid that out for you last night," I said. "I'm in this to the end of it, no matter what comes up along the way, if you level with me — and if you're clean. If you're not, the hell with you." I paused. "You'll have to admit you haven't given me much to work on."

He nodded. Then he brushed his hand over his hair, wincing just a bit when he rubbed the white patch over the lump, or what was left of it. "I do admit I have not told you everything. But I had good and sufficient reason for not doing so before, as I shall explain. I was merely protecting myself. And I had no idea whatever that such a tragic . . ."

He stopped and sighed, then went on briskly. "Last night shortly before nine P.M., Miss Antoinette burst into my office. She had a gun in her hand."

"She had a — wait a minute. Your receptionist told me nobody came in past her."

His face grew an expression of mild irritation. "Miss Prinz is not allowed to smoke in the office, but is a slave to nicotine." I had a hunch he didn't smoke. "She often goes to the ladies' rest room to satisfy her ungovernable craving. We both pretend I don't know about it I should guess she was smoking when Miss Antoinette came in. That is of no importance at the moment. Miss Antoinette *did* burst into my office, and she did have a gun in her hand." He stopped momentarily.

"O.K. Carry on."

"Miss Antoinette was in a perfectly frightful state. She had obviously been crying and was very distraught. She cried out something like, 'You monster, you criminal' — I'm not sure of the words. It was a moment of some confusion, and I admit to a feeling of apprehension at sight of the gun. Justifiable apprehension, as it turned out. She fired that gun at me."

"The hell she did."

Gordon Waverly looked at me with the air of one long suffering and, lapsing into the speech of the common man, said, "The hell she didn't. She tried to kill me."

Twelve

I said, "She took a shot at you here? In this office?"

"She did."

"Then there ought to be a bullet buried, if not in you, at least somewhere around the joint."

That flicker of mild irritation again. "Obviously, her aim was not perfect." He swiveled sideways in his chair and pointed. Once he pointed at it, the hole was quite apparent. A small dark spot in the center of one of the pale beige wall panels.

He said, "I am disappointed that a man so ready with large and even minute observations would fail to notice the spot where the bullet lay buried." But then he smiled. "Forgive me," he said. "I should not have indulged in the doubtful pleasure of sarcasm. But your manner, Mr. Scott, is — well, abrasive. At any rate, there is the hole. The bullet barely missed my head. Shall I continue?"

I grinned. "Please do."

"I was astonished. Needless to say — or perhaps I *should* say — I hadn't any idea what possessed the woman. I was, I'll admit, frightened. More precisely, I was petrified. If she had fired that infernal weapon again she might have hit me, and I should not now be telling you this. But she did not fire it. She swayed, then burst into sobs."

I got out a cigarette and stuck it between my lips, then remembered Waverly's comment about "slaves to nicotine," and glanced at him. He nodded. I had permission. I lit up and sucked smoke deep into my lungs. Maybe that was why Miss Prinz wasn't allowed to smoke. If she breathed any deeper than I'd seen her breathing last night, she'd have to buy a whole new wardrobe.

Waverly went on, "I was by then able to get up and approach her. I led her to a seat and managed to calm her somewhat. While sobbing and dabbing at her eyes, she told me that only an hour before she had been approached by a large and extremely unpleasant individual who had attempted to blackmail her. She had convinced herself that I had sent him. Or, if not I personally, that I was at least the individual responsible."

"Did she describe this guy? And was it anybody she knew?"

"She described him quite well, but it was no one she knew, nor did her description fit anyone with whom I am acquainted."

"O.K. Leave that for now. What did the guy have to bleed her with? That is, what did he know about Natasha that made him think she'd pay money to keep it hushed?"

"She had been going for some time with a married man. Early this month they were — hitting the jazz spots out of town, as she put it. It was late Saturday night, and they had drunk a good deal, especially the man. Returning to Los Angeles, her escort, who had been driving erratically, struck another auto from behind. The other car went out of control and off the road, crashing into a tree. Miss Antoinette's companion did not stop, but instead drove in great haste from the scene of the accident."

Waverly rested both hands on his desk and pressed the tips of his fingers together. "Now, the man who approached her last evening possessed this information. He claimed there had been a witness to the crime. However, Miss Antoinette insisted — to me, not to the man attempting extortion — that the driver of the other car could not possibly have seen them, and that the accident could hardly have been witnessed by anyone else. It occurred on Laurel Canyon Boulevard, and there was little illumination except that from the automobile's headlights. She insisted that, even had someone been nearby, he could not have seen the car's occupants, certainly not with enough clarity to identify them. She was quite positive about that. Therefore, she assumed the only possible explanation was — "

It hit me. "Wait a minute." I held up a hand to stop him. I got up, walked across the room and back. Then I turned and looked at Waverly. "Don't tell me Nat — Miss Antoinette — wrote a fool letter to Amanda Dubonnet."

He smiled again. "Marvelous. How did you deduce that?"

"Is that what happened?"

"It is."

"Damn her hide." I sat down again. "And I didn't just pull the deduction out of the air. A little while before Nat was shot she read a story in this morning's paper about your being held as a suspect in Pike's murder. That didn't set her off. But at the very bottom of the page was a line to the effect that Pike wrote the column 'Lifelines for the Lifelorn,' for *Inside*, under a pen name. The story was continued there, and it happened just before she turned the page, to where the pen name, Amanda Dubonnet, was given. When she read that bit about *Pike's* being the author of the letters-to-the-genius column, she keeled over. If she'd spilled the whole story to Pike — Amanda — in a letter, then told you, after taking a pot-shot at your head . . . Well, I'm starting to understand why she keeled over this morning. She must have thought her going to see you last night caused you to murder Pike. Not to mention the fact that she probably felt the whole scandal was going to blow up in her face."

Waverly nodded. "There is one other good reason why she might have fainted, Mr. Scott. If she believed I had murdered Mr. Pike, it is possible she felt I had lied to her last night, had then silenced Mr. Pike — and would thus soon have to silence her also."

"Uh-huh. Of course, she was wrong."

"Completely."

"*Did* Natasha spill all the beans in a letter to Amanda?"

"That is what she told me. Of course, she did not use her real name, but did include her real address. Which isn't surprising, really, since she had no reason to expect any action other than a letter from Amanda, or possibly a personal reply in the column — we receive hundreds of letters which can't be used in the column, you understand."

I nodded.

"As for the letter itself, it was several pages, I understand. She not only told of her involvement with this man, and of the hit-and-run accident, but said that she felt her escort should have stopped to give aid, and that she should inform the police of what had occurred. But she was also afraid she might herself be prosecuted, or jailed, in the circumstances. Her letter, I gather, was much like thousands of others we have received, a rather tortured outcry, and a plea for information and advice."

"You gather? You mean you don't really know what was in her letter?"

"I have not seen it. Mr. Pike would have received it."

"Ah."

"Do you begin to see — "

"Yeah. I do begin to."

I had not only begun to see, but Waverly's words were still going around in my head — "a letter much like thousands of others we have received . . . tortured outcry . . . plea for information and advice. . . ."

Waverly pulled at his lower lip. "You understand, Mr. Scott, Miss Antoinette's story did not unfold as I have been presenting it to you. It came from her in jerks, spasmodically, in bits and pieces — which, slowly, I put together into what I can only call an appalling pattern."

"Of blackmail. Letters to Amanda, then Amanda picks the ones most ripe for bleeding and sends his boy for the transfusion."

"The — yes. At first I understood only that Miss Antoinette had divulged in a letter to Amanda information which she should have entrusted only to the proper authorities, if to anyone. But you would not believe the secrets and confidences, and even confessions, which pour into a column such as 'Lifelorn'."

"Sure I would."

I was starting to light another cigarette, but I froze.

My lighter was low on fluid, and I just looked at the little flame until it petered out. Not until this moment had I thought about that handwritten page I'd picked up in the gutter across the street from Finley Pike's home. But I thought about it now.

Waverly said, "Is something wrong?"

"No, something's right. Have you got a match?"

He frowned. Maybe he didn't mind if I smoked; but clearly he didn't want actually to contribute to my delinquency. However, be found a book of matches in a desk drawer and handed it to me. The book carried advertising copy — advertising *Inside*. No clues there.

I lit my cigarette, and Waverly continued, "As I say, at first I knew only that Miss Antoinette was being blackmailed; I thought the information with which to blackmail her had been obtained from a letter she wrote to Amanda, and that she blamed me. It was immediately apparent that Miss Antoinette *must* be pacified or she might in her frenzy tell others her story. Tell, for example, others in the industry, or newspaper reporters . . . Whether there was any truth to her allegations or not, I knew it *must* not become even a rumor in Hollywood. That could of itself be fatal, could ruin *Inside*, my reputation, several reputations. You understand?"

"I begin to."

He pulled at his lip again. "I told Miss Antoinette I was totally innocent but would do all in my power to help her establish the facts, whatever they might be. If anyone on my staff was involved in an attempt to blackmail her he would be brought to justice. I then suggested we contact the police. And that diminished her hysteria considerably."

I blinked. "She wanted the cops in on it?"

"On the contrary. She preferred that the police know nothing about the affair. So, not only because an exploratory investigation did indeed seem advisable, but primarily to pacify Miss Antoinette, I suggested we employ, at my expense, a private investigator — of her choosing, to eliminate any suspicion that I might select one favorable only to my own interests. She mentioned your name, said she knew you. I asked her to place the call so she would be certain her choice had actually been telephoned."

"You weren't missing any bets, were you?"

"She . . . ah, still had the gun."

"Uh-huh. At the time I suppose she was pretty well shaken, maybe dripping a few late tears?"

"She had stopped actually sobbing and shrieking but was not back to normal by any means."

Which would explain why she'd sounded like a fish strangling in an aquarium. Waverly's story seemed, at least so far, to be plugging the holes I'd meant to probe.

He said, "For the same reason, I let her listen to my conversation with you. And she calmed down almost completely. Once calm, she related her story in such precise and exact fashion, and with such artlessness and sincerity, I became convinced she was telling me the truth. That accepted, I had to accept the logical corollary, that Mr. Pike had betrayed his confidence and was the true author of the blackmail. I believed he was blackmailing Miss Antoinette — and if her, why not another? A dozen others? Perhaps *several* dozens of others."

"Why not?"

"I almost became ill when the extensions of that thought became apparent. If he was engaged in blackmail of others, perhaps some of those others had guessed the information must have come from their letters to Amanda and — like Miss Antoinette — assumed erroneously that I myself was a party to the blackmail. It was that thought which sent me to Mr. Pike's home. I let Miss Antoinette out the side exit after telling her I would have you call upon her; I considered the situation briefly, then determined to have it out with Mr. Pike."

"And raced out of here yelling, 'Finley Pike! I'll fix him,' or words to that effect."

"Eh?" He frowned at me. "Oh, no. I couldn't have done anything like that. I was angry, of course . . . but, no."

"Miss Prinz might have garbled it a little."

"Well . . . the rest you know."

"So you went to Pike's and beat hell out of him."

"I did *not* — I repeat, Mr. Scott, the rest you know. All else occurred precisely as I told you."

"So why didn't you tell me last night about Natasha's flip? Why wait till now?"

He seemed truly surprised. "Why," he said, "I assumed that would be apparent to you at this point."

I blinked. And then realized he was right. "Yeah," I said "I'm a little slow. Motive, you mean."

"Certainly. The police were, and I'm sure still are convinced I murdered the man. They know I was there and that I knew the victim. But there is not any evidence that Mr. Pike and I were on anything but the best of terms. The truth is, we got along extremely well. The police have everything except a motive for the crime. If I had told them, or they had overheard me telling you, of Miss Antoinette's allegations — that I believed Mr. Pike to be engaged in a possibly enormous blackmail operation, an operation fed by information extracted from letters to the 'Lifelines for the Lifelorn' column in my journal, *Inside* — clearly my position would have been hopeless. Additionally, true or false, *that* would have been emblazoned in the newspaper stories this morning."

He'd called it a "journal." But he was right on the nut this time, too. The police would have had one hell of a motive — or, rather, their choice of two: Waverly, furious at the sudden revelation that Pike was using an *Inside* column for blackmail, raced to Pike's, beat him, and then killed him; or, Waverly was co-partner with Pike in the blackmail, there was a falling-out-among-thieves, and Waverly pounded on Pike and then killed him. Either way, my client would soon be inside looking out.

It also occurred to me that either of those motives would fit Waverly very nicely, if he *had* killed Pike. More, if his story was true, only Natasha Antoinette could have corroborated it. If he'd been lying to me, it was very convenient for him that she was now dead.

It was clear as mountain air, however, that either Waverly was telling me the truth or he was very, very clever.

I said, "O.K., Mr. Waverly, now explain away the connection between you and Al Gant and we'll be in business."

"There is no connection between me and Mr. Gant."

"I thought I told you — "

"Yes, you told me. That does not make it true. It could be true, though, I suppose. At least it's possible."

"What does that mean?"

"All I know is that Miss Willow and two other persons active in the industry — whom I respect, by the way — approached me something over two years ago and suggested that I was a suitable person to begin publishing a new Hollywood journal. They were willing to provide the necessary capital. The idea appealed to me and, after mulling over the offer for a few days, I accepted with pleasure. But where my associates — including Miss Willow — got their money, which they invested in the enterprise, I do not know. In fact, I never thought about it until now."

He placed his hands on the desk again, pushed his fingers together, and looked directly at me. "I have heard the name Al Gant, yes. But I have never met the man, have never been and am not now associated in any way with him. If you say that some of his criminal associates were at Mr. Pike's last night I will accept your statement. But that acceptance is not based on any knowledge of my own. I know nothing of this person, whoever it was, that the police shot last night at Mr. Pike's. I did not even know until you told me that anyone had been shot. Now, again, and for the last time in our discussions, I did not kill Mr. Pike."

Well, ambivalence will chop up an investigation eight ways from the middle. So either I told Waverly good-bye, or I went ahead on the assumption that he was as honest as the day is long, and it was the middle of summer. Besides, once you really make up your mind, a lot of the missing elements often fall magically into place. I made up my mind.

"O.K.," I said. "We're in business. So, by the numbers. One, if there's Gant money in your — your journal, slipped in by Miss Willow, I'll find out about it. Two, those hoods of Al's were sure as hell headed for Pike's last night — one of them went back — so if there's no connection between you and Gant it's better than eight to five there was some kind of link either between him and Pike *or* him and the guy who ruined Pike's brains. Three, if Natasha said there was no witness to that hit-run, I believe her — which means someone, probably Pike, had a blackmail bonanza going right here under your nostrils; if he was blackmailing other letter writers, I think I've got a hunk of one of those letters — though I didn't realize it till a few minutes ago — and I may be able to trace it to the writer, and thus to one more of the victims. . . ."

I stopped. It's funny how conviction sneaks up on you. In that moment I became completely convinced Waverly hadn't killed Pike. See? Magic. Nobody, but nobody, could have been *that* clever about it. So I went on, "Thanks to the unintentional helpfulness of Pike's killer, who must have dropped it after exiting in one hell of a hurry from the house. Four, fill me in on how the Amanda section operated and show me what files you've got here, give me Natasha's description of that would-be collector, supply any details you've got on the hit-run she told you about, and accept my abrasive apologies for leaning on you a mite — and I'll get out of here."

He grinned. It wasn't a mere smile this time but a real, big, grinny grin. "We," he said, "are in business."

Thirteen

After leaving Waverly I drove back to the Spartan. In my bedroom I found the coat I'd been wearing the previous night. The crumpled and soiled sheet of paper was in the pocket, where I'd stuck it.

The thing wasn't part of a story for *True Agony Confessions*, but it was true agony: one page of a letter, from one of the tortured ones Waverly had mentioned, to Amanda Dubonnet. At least, so I assumed; there was nothing on the sheet of paper, or in the lines written on it, to indicate that. But maybe between the lines there was.

Except that, when I'd read the whole sheet carefully, I still hadn't found a thing that might lead me to its writer, not a glimmer. At least nothing I could see. I read it over quickly three or four more times, then forgot about it. For the moment.

Then, back to my list, putting the lines out, phoning, seeing, talking — and this was the third time now. Lines out tagged, in addition to the others, Natasha Antoinette, Madelyn Willow — and Jeremy Slade.

Plus a description, and the question, "Who is he?" He being the blackmail boy, or bagman, the Collector. The description was all that Waverly had been able to give me from what Natasha, between or among sobs and shrieks, had told him: a big guy, not very clean, bald on the front of his head but with a kind of mound of hair, proceeding from the middle of his scalp on back, and in need of a cutting at the nape, maybe gray, maybe brown. For some reason she'd especially noticed his feet. As Waverly had recalled her colorful and somewhat jazzy word-picture of those extremities, they were "the biggest damn feet I ever did see, except on a hippopata-whatever the hell. Daddy, those were *feet*."

Not much. Maybe enough. So: a big lout, half bald, with feet that wouldn't quit. He'd called on Natasha at eight P.M. Before nine she'd been with Waverly.

I checked with the police. No help there, and no late developments. I did learn the brand of cigarettes Natasha's killer had smoked. Him and several million other people.

I talked to Madelyn Willow. She looked like the kiss-off of death, a gal at least a hundred and sixty years old, with a pound and a half of weight for each year, and two thirds of it fat. That's the way she looked. The sober truth was that she stood five feet, two inches tall and weighed one-ninety, which was a pretty sobering truth even without exaggeration. She had starred, about thirty years back, in a B-minus movie in which she kissed the male lead on the neck, and then bit him, and danced on tippy-toe at the New Year's Eve ball. It was hard to believe: She had danced on tippy-toe.

Al Gant? Who? Of course I don't know him, whoever he . . . Who? Aldo Gianetti? Is there something wrong with you, young man? Of *course* it was my money. I made thousands, millions, when I was a Star. I — what? Of *course* it was my own money; I told you I never heard of . . . I'll report you to the authorities, young man. I'll *report* you.

I told her, golly, I was only asking, and left, having learned exactly as much as I'd expected to: nothing. But there are ways and ways.

During the afternoon I kept thinking about Cherry Dayne. I called and talked to her twice, partly to see if she'd remembered anything about the rifleman, but also to tell her to keep under cover and not wander around where she, too, might get shot. The more I learned, or guessed, about this case the more concerned about Cherry I became.

Maybe I should have been worrying more about me.

It happened when I least expected it.

I might have been tailed from time to time during that afternoon — but not for long at a time, and I can say that without boasting. Watching for and avoiding a tail is simply routine, a fact of investigative life, part of the job; you'd expect a bookkeeper to know how to keep books. But, still, they could without too much trouble have gotten a line on what I was up to, on where I might go next or go at some time during the next hour or two.

It was nearly five P.M., and I'd spent the last couple of hours calling on members of Slade's production company, the cast and crew, hoping one of them — when alone, rather than among others who could overhear a comment — might have something to add to my fragments. But none of them had any more fragments. Anyone aware of what I was doing, though, could have assumed, logically enough, that I would eventually get around to calling on others of the company, certainly the principals, and could have chosen the spot accordingly, to lie in wait for me.

Yeah. Afterwards I figured it out. But to be sure of staying alive you've got to figure those things out *before*. So who's sure of staying alive?

For about twenty seconds I wasn't at all sure.

I'd parked at the curb on Palm Drive before the two-story Beverly Hills home of Vivyan Virgin. I got out of the car thinking that Vivyan was sure a lot of woman, and I like lots of women, and even if she couldn't help on the case I hoped she was home, and —

That was all the real thinking I did for a while.

I heard the whine of the slug whipping past my head before I heard the crack of the gun. It's funny what goes through your mind at a time like that. I was thinking: It's not the rifleman, at least not the same rifle, because I heard the shot — that, and possibly as many as eighteen other things. But I was not dwelling on any of these thoughts with real concentration, because I was spread-eagled in the air, having taken a leap that would have done credit to a large gazelle, and then I was skidding over Vivyan's lawn with my chin digging into it like a mole. But not for long.

I hit, felt the lawn shoving against my chin, then rolled over and over again, getting the .38 Colt Special into my hand between rolls. I got a foot planted firmly and shoved — but it slipped on the slick grass and went out from under me. And a good thing, too.

I'd heard a second shot, and as my foot slipped and I flopped on my chest again, the third slug raked my back. I felt my coat twitch as the bullet tore through it and the slicing burn as it raked the skin. A little lower and I might not have gotten up. But I got up, and this time my feet didn't slip.

I bent forward and sprinted toward Vivyan's house. The shot had come from my left, and I angled right, away from the man with the gun. I hadn't seen him, had only a general idea where he was, but several impressions had piled one on another in my brain, and I knew what I was going to do. If I didn't get hit.

There was one more shot, but it missed as I jumped past the side of the house, landing in some clipped shrubbery. There was one house beyond Vivyan's, on the corner lot at the intersection of two streets. The man was there somewhere, about a hundred feet away. The gun he was using had the solid, heavy sound of a .45 automatic, so it was a good thing none of those fat slugs had done more than scrape me. But I knew where he was and could guess he was either in or near a car, parked around the corner for a quick getaway. There was a chance he had company, another man or two with him; but he might be alone.

As I went past the side of Vivyan's house I caught its edge with my left hand and dug in my heels, jerked back and fired one shot from my .38 in the general direction of the corner, but high, so I wouldn't hit anybody. I didn't have a chance of potting the gunman and I didn't want to hit anybody else. The shot was just sound effects, anyway, to make the mugg think I was standing at the corner of the house. While the crack of my Colt was still echoing I turned and sprinted alongside the house, then left, behind it, toward that intersecting street.

There was a low brick wall between the two lots, and I went over it like a man taking a toy hurdle. My feet made little sound on the grass, which was also planted back here. Straight ahead of me was a car, a spic-and-span new Corvair, empty. It was the gunman's car. I didn't know that at first, but I did in the next few seconds.

My hope was that the bastard was still near the corner, waiting for me to poke my head around the side of Vivyan's house so he could blow some of it off. He wasn't. Knowing he'd missed me, he'd had enough; now he was going to get the hell out of the area and try another day. At least, that was obviously his idea.

I kept sprinting when I reached the sidewalk and turned left — and the big mugg was suddenly right in front of me, running toward his car, the heavy .45 still in his right hand. But the gun was angled toward the ground, and mine was up, held before me and all I had to do was swing it an inch to center it on his middle.

We saw each other at the same time, but there was a little difference. I had been expecting to see him. That little difference was enough. If we'd kept running we would have plowed into each other hard enough to knock us both silly, but we both tried to stop. I slapped my feet down on the sidewalk and skidded over the cement toward him, knees bent, as he let out a hoarse gasp of surprise and threw his gun hand up toward me.

As soon as I'd seen him and planted my feet I squeezed the trigger of my gun. The slug caught him high in the chest but didn't turn him. He jerked off one shot. The bullet hit the sidewalk yards past me and spun, whining, up off the cement. We were two feet apart when I squeezed off my second shot and then we collided, not gently. The bore of my Colt was against his belly, and I rammed it deeper into his gut and poured the third and last slug into him.

It was the impact of our bodies more than the bullets in him that sent him down. He fell on his side, gun clattering on the cement and bouncing away from him. He rolled, then struggled to a sitting position with both arms out, hands pressed against the sidewalk. For a second or two he sat there, blood beginning to well from the three holes in him, an expression of shock and bewilderment on his face.

Then he grunted, slumped forward, put his hands beneath him and pushed, got swaying to his feet. He was a big sonofabitch, a tough one — he had been a tough one. He lifted his arms, fingers opening and closing slowly. He wasn't reaching for me. He was just reaching — for something. His throat moved spasmodically. His mouth opened. He made a liquid choking sound, and thick blood gushed over his lips, smearing his chin.

He leaned forward and spat noisily — and then just flopped. As if he'd been hanging from a cord and the cord had been cut. He went down like a sack of meal, all his muscles emptied of life and strength in the same instant. His head thudded against the sidewalk. All his muscles relaxed; his bowels and bladder emptied; blood oozed from his mouth and formed an almost doughy puddle on the cement. It looked as if part of his lunch was mixed in with it. He lay there with his face on the cement, in his own blood and wastes.

Lesson for would-be killers: Either don't miss with your first shot, or else eat light, go to the john, take an enema, and be ready to die neat.

Ugly? Sure it was ugly. Violent death is always ugly. It isn't sugar and spice and turn to another channel. There are punks who think it's tough, manly, smart, to carry a gun or keep a switchblade on their hip. They should have seen the big boy go.

He was big, all right. Big, and bald in front. His collar wasn't just dirty, it was grimy. His feet were the tag. I wear a sizable shoe myself, but two of his would have made three of mine.

Daddy, those were feet.

Fourteen

I didn't just stand there staring at the dead man. I looked around for another live one. But apparently the big boy, the Collector, hadn't had a partner. I wondered at how many other places lone hoods might be sitting, waiting to see if I'd show up.

If I'd had time I would have gone visiting, to see if I could find any of them. But I didn't have time.

It had been perhaps half a minute since that first shot. The blast of a .45 carries a long way, and he'd triggered off five shots at me. Then there'd been four more from my Colt. Almost like a small war here, just off Palm Drive in Beverly Hills. And in Beverly Hills you're not even supposed to laugh loud enough to disturb the neighbors.

So, phones would have been ringing. I guessed that by now several dozen citizens had called, or tried to call, the law, and possibly even the fire department and the air force. Anyhow, already I could hear a siren.

The first movement I noticed was a little kid, a boy about six years old standing ten feet from me — me and the one on the sidewalk. He was in blue jeans, a torn white T shirt, and tennis shoes.

"Geez," he said.

"Go on, kid," I said. "You shouldn't be out here."

He swallowed and looked at me, then at the dead man. "Boy," he said. "Is he dead?"

"He's dead. Now beat it. Go on home to your mother."

Kids, at least till they're six or eight years old, have a different attitude toward life — and death — a view uniquely their own. We lose it as we get older. Maybe we get wiser; maybe we just lose our innocence. But at five or six or eight, there's a naturalness that's too soon gone.

This one looked up from the dead man. "Did he get sick?" he asked soberly.

"Yes, a little. But he'd been sick a long time. Go on home, son."

He turned, looked back. "Boy," he said, and ran.

But by that time I was under the eyes of several adults. Their eyes held no innocence. But they held a lot of consternation — and condemnation. They didn't know who'd fired the first shot, or why. But they knew I'd killed a man. And that was bad. More, this was Beverly Hills, and I had littered the streets. I had brought an obscenity into their lives.

I ignored two or three comments. But then a woman about thirty, in tight slacks and gold shoes with four-inch heels somewhat thicker than twopenny nails, gasped, "How ghahstly, how harrible!" Some playing cards, probably a bridge hand, were still clutched in her fingers. Then she said to me, "You — you *killed* him. *You* killed him."

I almost mentioned a word which is generally unmentionable. Here I had been shot at five times and — don't ask me how — had been missed five times. Except for that one; except for the furrow on my back, still burning. I wasn't any happier than these people were; I hadn't enjoyed it, either. It was just possible I had enjoyed it less.

I should have kept my mouth shut. I didn't. I said truthfully, "Yeah. He spat on the sidewalk."

She started to bark something else at me. Then she stopped. Then she got sort of pale green. Then she left. One down, and a million to go. But the siren was now a low crooning sound nearby, and in a moment the radio car stopped near me at the curb.

There were the police, then home to the Spartan to shower — easy on the back — and change clothes again, so it was seven o'clock before I got back to Vivyan's.

I was not in the best mood of my life, not even the best of my day. It is, therefore, quite a tribute to Vivyan Virgin that, approximately four and one half seconds after she opened her front door, I was feeling pretty jazzy. She delicately patted a real, or feigned, yawn. She stretched like a cat half asleep in the sun. She moved her shoulders slowly, deliciously back and forth, just a bit, the way bears scratch their backs on trees, only not nearly so ferociously.

"Oh-hh-hhh-hh," she said. "Hmmmmm-mm," she said. "Oh, mmm, hello. I was taking a nap." She smiled sleepily. "When the chimes rang. So I jumped out of bed and just threw on this old peignoir."

Didn't look so old to me.

"Well, you're Mr. Scott, aren't you? Shell Scott?"

With my tongue behind my front teeth I whistled one of those thin little whistles. "*Tweee-wee-ooo.*" I didn't mean anything by it. Frankly, I didn't know I was whistling. In fact, I didn't know I could whistle like that.

"You are Mr. Scott, aren't you?"

"*Twee-wee-ooo.*"

Boy, Jeremy Slade and I should get together, I thought. He could tweet to me, and I could answer. We might wind up building a nest. Finally, though, I found my tongue. It was right there behind my front teeth.

"Yessss," I said.

"Would you like to come inside?"

"I'm sure not going to stand out here."

She turned and walked away from me, leaving the door open, and I followed, bumping into the door jamb and cracking my elbow rather severely.

Kids, hold on. Don't jump to the conclusion that old Scott is over the hill, or under it, or anywhere near it. But you should have seen that big, busty, flamboyant blast of a babe, Vivyan Virgin, standing there in the doorway going "Ohh-hh-hhh, hmm, mmmm," and all the other things she said. In that peignoir she mentioned. Which was hardly worth mentioning. Besides, it was the same color as her skin. I know, because you could see her skin through it, and it was exactly the same color. She said she'd jumped out of bed and put on the peignoir, and it was apparent she slept in the raw. Though I don't know why anybody would call it "raw." Sure didn't look very raw to me.

So my thoughts went. All the way into the living room. She patted a chair, indicating I could sit in it, then she walked about ten feet past it to a long, low divan on which were piled at least a dozen satin-covered pillows in every color of the spectrum.

She didn't sit, she reclined on it. Like Cleopatra on Antony. Then she drew up her legs a mite, arranged them on the divan and pillows, fluffed her skin — that is, her skin-colored peignoir — leaned back, got comfy, and then said, "I really should change into something more hostessy, if you've got time."

"Baby, I don't have *that* much time."
"Well, now. Hello."
"Hi."
"What did you want to see me about, Mr. Scott?"
"Shell."
"You wanted to see me about Shell?"
"Shell — that's me."
"You wanted to see me about — you?"
"Uh. Not before I came in. I wanted to see you about something else then."
"Something else? What was it, Mr. Scott?"
"Shell."
"Shell?"
"Yeah. That's my name. Call me Shell."
"All right. Shell."

We sat there. Seconds ticked away. Time — valuable time — passed. Sometimes it's hard to get right down to work. You can understand that, can't you? I hitched my chair a couple feet closer to that Antony-type barge she was sailing on. I could imagine wind ruffling her hair. Brawny oarsmen pulling at brawny oars. Maidens dancing and throwing rose petals all over. You'd be surprised what I could imagine. Seconds ticked away.

"Oh, I remember," she said.
"How in hell could you remember? I just now thought of it."
"What you were saying. You said you wanted to see me about something else."
"Yes. Yes. I remember that, myself."
"What was it?"
"It was . . . something else."
"Don't you remember?"
"It'll come back to me."
"Well, let's talk about something else, then."
"That makes sense."
"The reason I was taking a nap — usually I don't — was because of all the excitement here this afternoon. Guns, and bullets, and a man killed right outside my door practically. Did you hear about it?"
"I was . . . one of the first to know."
"Wasn't it awful?"

"Terrible."

"Especially in Beverly Hills."

"It's against the law in Beverly Hills."

"Oh, it must be."

"I gather you didn't go out and look at all the excitement, and people, and blood, and . . . ugh."

"Goodness, no! I don't like to look at things like that."

"You darling, you."

"But I heard all about it from my neighbor. One horrible man shot another horrible man."

"Yeah."

"Then he stood over him shooting him, and looking wild."

"And snorting and panting and pulling gobs of hair out of his ears."

"I didn't hear about that."

"Give your neighbor a little more time."

"She was playing bridge — "

"Not *that* one!"

"And this horrible man — "

"Don't tell me. If I were you, I'd move."

"But I'm so comfortable. Why don't you come over here instead?"

I damn near did. I sprang to my feet with a gay "Why not?" on my lips, but a little voice inside me kept saying over and over, *Are you out of your mind?*

"Just a minute," I said.

I walked across the room, found a window, and opened it. I stuck my head out in the air and breathed a lot of it. I think she had ether piped into that room, or the scent of Midsummer Night's Madness, or something equally heady, but probably ether. It was one of those ether-or rooms. When that thought bloomed in my head like a rare weed, I figured it must be pretty clear again, so I pulled it back into the living room, walked back to my chair, pushed the chair a couple of feet over the carpet to where it had been originally, and sat down, while that little voice said, *Yes, you ARE out of your mind.*

"Miss Virgin," I said, and stopped. "Do I *have* to call you Miss Virgin?"

"Don't you dare."

"Don't I dare what?"

"Call me Miss Virgin."

"O.K. Vivyan."

"Shell."

It was starting again. I shook my head till my teeth rattled. Either it was my teeth, or else something new was loose. Besides Vivyan. This had to stop. We had to get on the ball here, on the track, get this show on the road. Life is real, life is earnest, we couldn't fritter it away like this.

"We're frittering it away," I said.

"Frittering what? And what's frittering, anyway? If it's what it sounds like, we haven't frittered it at all yet."

"Sure we — hold it. Hold everything."

"Shell."

"This has got to stop, Vivyan. We could go crazy like this. Mad. We could lose our marbles. Now listen closely. I am Shell Scott and — "

"I know that. And you told me."

"Will you shut — ah, Vivyan. Just listen to me for a minute, huh? I'm a private detective. I'm working on a case. I was. I am. Now, here's the way it is. . . ."

Well, things didn't really get on the track for a little while, but finally the conversation was almost lucid. And we were making some headway.

When I started to talk about my presence on location this morning, the memory of Natasha's death sobered Vivyan, and I was able to discuss the case with her. Only, she didn't have any idea who might have killed Natasha, or why, and said she even found it difficult to realize she was really dead.

"Well, she is, that's for sure," I said finally. "And it was cold-blooded murder." I hesitated. I didn't want to spill any of the beans about Finley Pike's possible blackmail operation — which, naturally, Waverly wanted me to keep under wraps as long as possible — but if Vivyan knew anything about the pressure on Natasha, I wanted to dig it out of her before she started sailing on that barge of hers again.

So I said, "You talked to Natasha on location this morning, didn't you?" She nodded.

"Did she mention being in any trouble?"

"What kind of trouble?"

"Well . . ." I hesitated again, then went on, "Did she say anything to you about somebody trying to blackmail her?"

She leaned back against the cushions behind her — she'd been sitting up for a while, which had probably helped keep the conversation in conversational channels — and said, "Goodness, no. Was somebody?"

"Actually, I'm not certain. Put it this way: did she tell you anything about a big, grimy character, half bald, heavy, giving her a hard time?"

She looked left, over my shoulder, and blinked, "What did he look like?"

I repeated the description Waverly had given me, plus details I'd gathered from personal observation. She said, "It doesn't ring any bells in me, Shell. Natasha didn't mention anybody, much less someone like that. Oh, she seemed under a strain, and nervous, but I thought that was because she was getting ready for the death dance, and — "

She kept rattling on, but I let my mind wander. This was the longest consecutive string of words to come from Vivyan yet, and some of it was near-babbling. Something had happened when I'd described the Collector. There'd been a reaction I hadn't expected — and didn't understand. "It doesn't ring any bells in me," she said. Maybe; but there'd been some kind of tinkle. She was still talking. ". . . Of course, it's going to stop shooting for a while, too — poor Jerry, he lost all that money when I was out sick, and now there's this terrible thing. Of course, Natasha *had* finished her last scene, except for the execution when they cut off her head, but they can use a double for that, but Jerry must be broken up a lot anyway. Not the money, but because of Nat. They were pretty thick the last few weeks, you know — of course, he's married, but it's not one of those 'till death do us — '"

"*Hold* it," I said.

She stopped. She'd been staring past my shoulder again and she jumped a little, then brought her gaze back to me. I even looked around myself, to make sure there was nothing extraordinarily interesting back there, but there wasn't. Merely the wall and, closer to me of course, my shoulder. Vivyan simply hadn't been looking at my face.

The artificial flow of words, more like a nervous reaction than a conversational response, had begun when I'd asked about, and described, the Collector, the guy I'd shot here a couple of hours or so ago — but Vivyan had told me she didn't know anything about that except what her neighbor had passed along, didn't know who'd been involved in the shooting. Funny. If she *had* known, I wondered why she'd pretended not to.

But I let it ride for the moment, and said instead, "Vivyan, you have finally said not merely one but about six things that interest me immensely. Maybe if we take them one at a time, instead of lickety-split all at once —"

"I'm sorry," she interrupted. "I guess I was kind of rattling on."

"What's this about Slade and Nat being pretty thick?"

"They'd been seeing each other some for the last few weeks; didn't you know?"

"Nope."

"I don't guess it was any secret. Nat talked to me about it. She liked Jerry a lot."

"Yeah? And Jerry?"

"Well, it was a pretty big thing — I guess it went both ways. It usually does, doesn't it?"

"I thought Nat and Ed Howell were a big item."

"Oh, they were. Still are, I guess — I mean, would be if she hadn't been . . . if it hadn't happened this morning." She paused and shrugged prettily. "No reason a girl has to have just *one* man, is there? A single girl, anyway. Like me."

That was right, she was single again. Husband number four, I recalled, was in Acapulco, drowning his sorrows and lying in the sun, getting his tan back. I pressed Vivyan for details about the "thing" between Slade and Natasha, but there wasn't anything she could add.

"That was Natasha's last important scene? The death dance?"

"Yes, except for the one where Gruzakk cuts off her head with his sword. But they wouldn't really *show* that, anyway."

I knew. They wouldn't actually *show* it, not *quite*. And you wouldn't actually *see* the head pop off and roll about like a cabbage, but you'd think you were *going* to see it. That was the technique Slade usually employed, and it had proved effective. And profitable. And, of course, tremendously nauseating.

Profitable. Yes, finally; though it had been a tight squeak for a while. "It looks as if the last *Goo* film may clean up now," I said. "But Slade was pretty close to the edge, wasn't he? You mentioned being out of the film for a while. . . ."

"When I was sick, yes."

It was difficult to think of this gal as ill. If she was as healthy on the inside as she looked on the outside, I gave her another hundred years of vigor. I grinned. "You look healthy as vitamins to me," I said, hoping she'd pick it up. She did.

"Oh, it wasn't anything re*pulsive*," she said. "It didn't affect . . . I mean, it wasn't anything like hives or — oh, it was more like heebie-jeebies. I was blowing my lines, and I couldn't concentrate. Got to feeling creepy. So I stayed home a few days, then started going to an analyst." I have pretty firm ideas about a number of things, one of them being psychoanalysis. But among the natives it isn't considered jolly to poke pins in the witch doctor, so I merely said, "Better heebie-jeebies than hives. I would have sworn you didn't have a heebie in you."

It must have struck the right note, because she smiled joyously and said, "Thanks. I'm lots better already, and Dr. Macey says he can cure me completely in four or five years."

"That's grand. Good for Dr. Macey. He's your analyst?"

"Yes. Of course you've heard of him?"

"Nope. I'm not exactly a fan — "

"He's one of the top two or three in all of Beverly Hills."

Which meant that, among his kin, he was at the head of the family. There are in Beverly Hills more psychoanalysts per convolution than in any other spot in the world. I'm not sure, but I think there are more analysts there than barbers. Which may be another item of fascination to future historians.

But we seemed to be getting a bit off the track again, and with Vivyan the straight and narrow was the only road which led away from shambles. So I said, "How badly was Slade hurt when he had to hold up shooting?"

"Well, he ran out of money, you know. He was sort of gambling we'd make it on schedule, or maybe a day or two over. But his credit's good, I guess. Anyway, I understand his bank gave him gobs more."

"What bank is that?"

"I don't know. Who cares? Just a bank. Everything worked out all right, that's the important thing. I felt just terrible, anyway."

"Yeah. If he'd gone bust, there'd have been no more *Creeping Goo*." Which, I thought — but didn't add — might have been the greatest blow struck at juvenile delinquency since the abandonment of woodsheds.

We talked another minute or so, then I told her I'd better get on my way.

"Oh, don't," she said. "Not yet. It's been so much fun talking to you." She was looking past my shoulder again. And that little peculiarity intrigued me.

The more you interrogate people for a purpose and try to separate truth from falsehood, the more you look for and hope for the little giveaways, the personality tip-offs. They're not too easy to find, but once found they can be pure gold.

As: Once, in a table-stakes poker game with five other men, when I was very nearly down to the table, I became aware that every time one heavy bettor ran a bluff he cleared his throat before announcing his bet. That little "ahem" made me well.

Or, take the wife of a man I was trying to find. She was an apparently honest but extremely nervous gal, and every time she lied she giggled. I simply checked the giggles and found hubby.

Those happy discoveries are seldom so easily made, and the tips are seldom so obvious. But I felt pretty sure that here again was a nugget — in Vivyan's occasional over-my-shoulder glances.

So I chatted casually for two or three minutes and then, without changing my tone at all, changed the subject a lot.

She was half smiling, relaxed, gazing at me with heavy, almost slumberous lids drooping over her eyes, when I said, still casually, "This big, half-bald guy I mentioned, the one I said might have been giving Nat a hard time, why did you tell me you hadn't heard of him?"

"Why, what do you mean? I don't understand — "

It was almost perfect. She remained completely relaxed, at least on the outside; she didn't even blink; her eyes stayed sleepy-looking — but they weren't on my face any longer. They even missed my shoulder this time, straying clear off course, way over to the vicinity of a potted plant or something.

I broke in, "Maybe it's none of my business, but if it is I'll dig around till I get the truth, somewhere else if I can't get it from you. And you know the boy I mean, Vivyan. The grimy slob needing a haircut, the guy I shot this afternoon practically on your doorstep, the citizen with big feet — "

Something had happened.

It jarred me; it wasn't part of the pattern.

She wasn't looking at the wall but straight at me. Her eyes were wide, staring.

And in staccato, disconnected little groups of words she was saying, "Shot? Shot him — he's dead? Dead? *You* shot him? You were the — then that's — Oh, thank God."

I sat there like a piece of furniture. Except for my jaw, which was sagging.

She had sat up straight and was breathing rapidly and deeply. Her breasts rose and fell under the transparent pink cloth, rose and fell at least six inches, a phenomenon which I would have considered worthy of real attention at any other time.

But this time I looked at her face as she leaned forward, clasping her hands tightly together, and said once again, "Oh, thank God."

Fifteen

Silence.

I could hear her breathing. The big, firm breasts rose and fell, rose and fell, slowing down. Or slowing up. Anyway, slowing.

I pulled up my jaw.

Then she said it quietly and simply.

"He was blackmailing *me*. Is he really dead?"

"There's no doubt about it." I got out a cigarette, lit it "Blackmailing you?"

"Yes."

"For how long?"

"Six months. It started almost six months ago. I haven't told anybody; I couldn't . . . God, what a relief."

It occurred to me that, if a gal was being blackmailed, and for good reason, that might be enough all by itself to send her into analysis. But there were too many more intriguing angles for me to think about that one.

I said, "How did he get his hooks into you? What did he have on you — or is that none of my business?"

"It's none of your business," she said, but she smiled to take the bite out of the words. "It's — oh, I didn't kill anybody, or steal anything. I didn't commit any — crime. It's just something, a lot of things, I don't want people to know about. I sure wouldn't want it in the papers or made public."

She paused, thinking, and unconsciously reached up and cupped her left breast in a long-fingered, red-tipped hand, and rubbed gently. She didn't actually cup it, since there was quite a lot that wouldn't fit in the cup. But there I was, losing the thread again.

Vivyan's words brought me back to the business at hand. More accurately, the business at foot, the big-footed blackmailer and where he fit into this case. She was saying, "If he's dead — well, *you* wouldn't blackmail me anyway." She smiled again. "One thing, there was a party up on Crescent Drive one night. Fourteen of us there. It was pretty wild. Somebody said the only thing wrong with nudist camps was they were so fouled up by nature."

"Nature?"

"The outdoors — mosquitoes, sunburn, and so on. You were always stepping on prickly things in the grass. And it was cold as Alaska some nights."

"I'll bet."

"Anyway, we decided to have an indoors nudist camp."

"*Fourteen* of you?"

"Fourteen. All fourteen — fourteen drunks. You can imagine."

"Yeah, you've got to watch that drinking — "

"That was about a year ago — some people were there you'd know if I mentioned their names, which I won't. We, well, we all went to camp for two or three months, then dissolved the group sort of automatically."

Went to camp, she said. Now whenever I thought of Boy Scouts and other jolly little kiddies "going to camp," Vivyan's words were going to fly into my mind like jaybirds.

"Well, hell," I said, "so you were all naked as — as jaybirds. But even fourteen of you, a whole flock, so what? That is, so what as far as blackmail's concerned. Maybe you were misguided, horribly abandoned, naughty even, but it's not likely you'd be sent to Folsom for twenty years — "

"Of course not. But if it was public knowledge, names and everything, it would be a mess, all right. Besides, that's just *one* of the things the man found out about me." She shook her head. "He really did a job on me. But I'd like to know who told him about that party." Then she took a breath and sighed, as if relaxing some more, and said, "Anyway, that was just one of the things he threw at me. I just told you about that to give you an idea."

"It gave me an idea. This guy, he had quite a bit more than that on you, huh?"

"Quite a bit."

I finally asked the question which had been on my mind for a while. Though I figured I knew the answer. "Vivyan, did you, by any chance, ever write a letter to Amanda Dubonnet? To *Inside's* 'Lifelines for the Lifelorn' column?"

She laughed, really amused. "You can't be serious. Why would I do a thing like that?"

Wrong again, I thought. And I also thought: What the hell? If she really hadn't written to Amanda, then what?

She was saying, "Why in the world did you ask me that, Shell?"

"Just . . . an idea."

"Pretty silly idea." She pretended to pout. "Do you really think I'm one of those idiots?"

"Not all of the people who write to Amanda are idiots, Vivyan. Some of them are intelligent enough, but maybe confused. Or lonely, scared, who knows? For some a letter to Amanda is probably a kind of catharsis more than anything else."

She had an odd look on her face. "Amanda," she said. "Of course. I read in the newspaper . . . That was Pike or something, the one who got killed last night. Wasn't it?"

I nodded. "Well, forget that. Vivyan, I hate to mention this, but how do you know that big guy was the only person involved?"

"He said he was. I never saw anybody else."

"What if he had a partner, or someone else knows the same info he knew? If so, just because he's dead it doesn't mean your troubles are automatically over."

We were quiet for a while; both of us had a lot to think about. But after a minute or two I stood up.

"I do have to go, Vivyan. I hope the big ape was the only one."

She tried on a smile. "If another comes around I'll tell you about it, and you can shoot him."

I grinned. "I can't promise, unless — like the joker today — he's shooting at me first."

"I'll arrange it."

On that point, with both of us greatly cheered, I left.

Jeremy Slade lived about three miles from Vivyan's place, and I drove straight there, without calling him first.

I dislike unannounced drop-ins, myself — they too often catch you with ten o'clock shadow, or enjoying a tasty dish, or at mealtime —

but that was precisely why I hadn't announced myself. A maid let me in, thus largely eliminating any chance of my catching Slade, figuratively speaking, with his pants down instead of his guard up, so I told her who I was and that I hoped to see Mr. Slade.

She showed me into a room that looked like a combination den and library, with animal heads and large, dead-looking fish mounted on the walls between bookcases. In about a minute Slade came in, the floor quivering a bit under his two hundred or so pounds.

"Mr. Scott," he said pleasantly, extending his hand. "It's good to see you."

I half doubted that, but he sounded sincere. At least, as sincere as that surprisingly wee voice of his could convey.

"Good evening, Mr. Slade," I said. "This is probably the unforgivable *faux pas*, but I was nearby and thought of a few things I wanted to ask you."

"It's quite all right. I suppose it's about Nat? I was just thinking about that terrible moment this morning. When she was killed." He swallowed, scowling as usual, but scowling gravely. There did, really, seem to be deeper lines in his squashed face, marks of fatigue and perhaps sorrow.

"What makes you think it's about Miss Antoinette?" I asked him.

He seemed surprised. "I don't know what else it could be. As I recall, you wanted to talk to her this morning."

"That's right. But I didn't quite make it."

"What was it you wanted to see her about, Mr. Scott?"

"It's not very relevant now that she's dead. Her death was quite a blow to me, personally. But even worse for you, I imagine."

"That's not important. The effect of Nat's death on the movie doesn't matter. Actually, we can still finish, but even if we had to scrap all we've shot it wouldn't be important compared to the tragedy."

"I wasn't thinking of the film, but your personal feelings about Natasha. I know you were close friends. Or, rather, quite a bit more than close friends."

It was hard to tell if he was glaring at me or just relaxing. "What the hell does that mean?" he said.

"Relax," I said, in case he wasn't really relaxing. "I heard you and Natasha were getting along very, very well lately, that's all."

"See here, Scott, I'm a married man."

"Hell, I wasn't talking to your wife."

Yeah, he was glaring. And scowling and doing a couple of other menacing things with his thick lips, and eyes, and eyebrows, and a little wiggle of his nose, too. He was still standing about six feet from me, but I could see all of that clearly enough.

"I might just walk over there and knock you on your can," he said.

"Look, if I'm off base, if it's really true there was nothing between you and Nat but chumminess and friendship, I apologize. But she's dead, and I liked her; and if necessary before I'm through I may ask half the people in town embarrassing questions. Including Jeremy Slade. Now, if you want to try pounding on me for a while, be my guest."

He'd lifted his hands up from his sides a few inches and balled them into shockingly formidable looking fists. The thought of "pounding" on somebody made me think of Pike's appearance last night, and for the hell of it I took a good look at Slade's knuckles and fingers. But they weren't banged up at all — not yet, anyhow.

Slowly he unwound the fists and let his arms drop to his sides again. Still glaring, and flaring his nostrils menacingly, he said, "I'll bet you get hit one hell of a lot."

I didn't say anything. The fact is, I do get hit more often than I like.

After a second or two, and a small snort, Slade went on, "To satisfy your damn inquisitiveness, Nat and I were friends, yes. That's all."

"You never went out with her? Partied it up? Had little tête-à-têtes in dimly lighted — "

"You must *want* to get dumped on your can," he interrupted. "Listen, the answer to all of that is no. N-O, no. Sure, I stopped in to see her a time or two — last night, in fact. But what the hell do you think a producer is? Just a guy who digs up some money? Don't I wish it! I got to be baby sitter, mother, father, child substitute — hell, half these people are like children themselves. I got to chuck them all under the chin once in a while."

"You saw Nat last night?"

He shrugged. "Yeah, yeah. She called me, said she was sick, afraid she couldn't work. Something's been squeezing her for a month or so. Hell, her big scene was coming up today, the death — the dance. So I chucked *her* under the chin, pumped her up, told her she was the greatest actress since Marie Dressler — "

"Marie Dressler?"

"And that she could make Salome look like Sophie Tucker — the same old oil. They know it's oil, but they can't live without it. They live *on* it. Hell," he grumbled happily, "I got to be a combination of Svengali and Norman Vincent Peale. Not to mention digging up the money."

"Speaking of money, who's your banker? He strikes me as a guy I'd like to do business with myself."

"Huh?"

"Well, he must be one of the friendliest bankers in town. He bailed you out when Miss Virgin held up the show last time, didn't he?"

"The hell he did."

"He didn't?"

"Hell, no. I thought I was going to damn near go broke for a while there, but Virge came back just in time." He shrugged those big shoulders again. "I managed to make it without borrowing any more." He lifted his lips away from his teeth, then slid them down again. He was a sight, I'll tell you. "It meant we had to rush the last half a little," he admitted, "but we got most of the scenes in the can with one take."

I guessed Vivyan had given me a bum steer or two. Maybe Slade was telling me the truth — I'd thought the last half of *Ghost of the Creeping Goo* seemed a little jerky. But that didn't prove anything; I'd thought the first half seemed a little jerky.

"Incidentally," I said, "when you saw Natasha last night, did she mention what was bothering her? I mean, any specific thing?"

He looked at me for a while, trying to hide his eyes under his eyebrow. "Just that she was sick, nerves were shot. I figured it was likely pre-menstrual fits, or maybe she was having her damn period. Hell, she's a woman; could've been one of several thousand ailments."

I nodded in silent agreement.

"I don't ask what ails them any more. Sometimes they tell me."

"You remember what time it was when you dropped in on her?"

This time he looked at me a bit longer. Then, "What the hell difference does it make?"

"It would satisfy my curiosity."

"I don't give a damn about your curiosity."

"You don't remember what time it was, huh?"

"Matter of fact, I don't. I was going over a script — stinking lousy script — when she called. I dropped it and drove over. I don't know what time it was." He looked at the wall, his face agonized in thought. "It was still daylight. Probably six, seven, somewhere around there. Hell, I don't know."

He pulled his eyes away from the wall and put them on me. "Let's knock this off," he said. "What was it you wanted to see me about?"

"That's all."

"That's . . . all? What the hell do you mean?"

"I mean, that's all," I said. "Thanks, and good night."

He stood there like a captive ape miraculously transported outside his cage. Suddenly among his tormentors, the little peanut-eating people. His hands closed and opened. His eyes virtually disappeared beneath his eyebrow. He peeled his lips up and ground his teeth together as if getting tartar off them, or trying to use them up. His hands closed and opened again.

As I walked past I sort of circled around him. No sense getting close enough so he could grab me. Don't get me wrong. I wasn't afraid of him. Not exactly. I'm not afraid of dying, either. Really I'm not. It's just that there are lots of things I'd rather do.

I let myself out and closed the door gently behind me.

Sixteen

I drove back toward Hollywood, top down on the Cad and wind scrubbing my face. I was thinking about the interesting interview just concluded. Interesting and, I believed, profitable.

Slade hadn't once asked me to sit down, I realized. He hadn't been the perfect host. Which, I guess, made us about even. I hadn't been the perfect guest, either.

I wondered if Slade had been telling me the truth or if he'd been giving me an artistic — more, a truly masterful — snow job. If snow, then he was a lot better actor than producer. One *hell* of a lot better actor than producer. He should have been starring in the *Goos*. As chief monster. Even as the hero, if he was that good.

I had to admit he'd come out of the interview in excellent shape. Which meant maybe Vivyan Virgin was mistaken about many things or was feeding me phonies. Well, time would tell. Time, and the rest of the pieces when fitted together. So I climbed into the Cad and drove off to do some more fitting.

Which thought made me wonder if Slade was still fitting — that is, continuing his fit or whatever he'd been building up to. Or was he slapping his thigh and laughing? I really would have liked to know. Even then I knew that was one of the important answers.

Back at my apartment I hung my jacket in the closet. It was part of my third change of clothes today — had to take care of the garments; this case was raising hob with my wardrobe.

As I swung the door shut, the mirror affixed to it caught the reflection from another mirror propped against the wall, and it gave me a dizzy moment.

A few days before — actually, it was at night — I had cracked the full-length mirror on the closet door. Never mind how I cracked it; that is not germane. Germane is the fact that a day or two later I picked up an even larger, man-sized job, and some of those little clamp things and screws, so that with a little mechanical wizardry and positive thinking I could put the mirror on the closet door myself. The enterprise would require positive thinking because, while I am a very lucky fellow, a dark fate seems to hang over my do-it-yourself jobs like a malevolent cloud, as if in compensation for other luckinesses. Skip the times I blew fuses, broke circuit breakers, taught a toilet to unflush; the point is, all these things were *challenges*. I could hire a man to fix my closet-door mirror, but it would be an admission of defeat. You can't let inanimate things lord it over you; if you do, they soon start laughing at you dumbly, and then you *are* in a fix. Then they don't live in your world, you live in theirs; they've got you.

No, though I might crack another mirror or two before I was through, and bark a thumb, and fly into maniacal rages, I would not hire the man; I would, for probably no more than three or four times what he'd charge me, do it myself. Then, whenever I looked at myself in my mirror — the hell with it.

What caused the dizzy moment was this: With the closet door at an angle it caught my reflection in the other mirror slanted against the bedroom wall. The latter was so slanted, with its base a foot or two out on the carpet, that my reflection was not only of me from the side, looking away from me, but apparently floating at an angle in the air below as if about to spring up at me.

Now, we rarely see ourselves as others see us, that is, in profile or from the back or screwed sideways. Think about it. At least, we don't unless we're expecting to see such a reflection, as in a tailor's three-mirrored booth.

And we almost *never* see us thusly and, in addition, floating slanted in the air as if about to spring up at us.

It was the first time for me.

I hope to hell it's the last.

It didn't help that I'd just come from watching Slade apparently giving birth to something large and jagged.

My first thought was, "Who is *that* ox?"

My second was, "Damn, I better kill it."

I actually yanked out my gun and very nearly ruined my do-it-yourself job before it even got started.

I might have done it too, except that the ox also yanked out a gun and pointed it — but away from me, and up into the air.

Of course, then I knew what had happened. I had a little laugh at myself. I was immediately back to normal.

I waggled my gun. He waggled his. I waved, he waved. I peeled my lips up and slid them down and ground my teeth together and stuck my tongue *way* out. Yeah, it was me. Or I. It was both of us.

Just a reflection of a reflection, that was all. But I breathed a lot easier when he put his gun away. Then I went into the kitchenette and mixed myself a dark, dark bourbon and water. You should have seen him peeling up his lips and grinding his teeth and all.

After a healthy belt, I carried my drink over to the divan, propped my feet on the squat and scarred coffee table, and picked up the telephone. There was checking to do with the people on my list, finding out if any of them had picked up an item or word I could use, and adding a few more requests and suggestions to my previous ones. I had about an hour on the phone ahead of me.

At three places my contact was out, and at each I left word for him to call back. I didn't say who was calling, but did leave the number of my bedroom phone — the unlisted one — and said I would be at that number for the next hour. Nearly all my contacts already had that number and thus would know who had called, but — I hoped — nobody else would. Just about the only people who have that unlisted number are crooks and girls. You can imagine how suspenseful it is when I'm awakened at two or so in the morning, when the bars have just closed.

After twenty minutes nothing of interest had developed, but that's often the way it is. A lot of any investigator's time is spent on the phone. Sometimes it's simply routine work that has to be done, but once in a while a single call saves fifty miles of legwork or even breaks a case.

So I took the last swallow of my drink and reached for the phone again. And the bedroom phone rang. Zip, I'd bounced up and over the back of the divan while it was still clanging, four big bounds and I was in the bedroom, and I plucked up the receiver in the middle of the second ring. If nothing else, that phone would help to keep me in shape.

"Hello," I said.

The voice wasn't one I'd expected to hear. It was bright and bubbly, and it said, "Shell? Hi, this is Cherry."

"Well, hello."

"What are you doing?"

I winced slightly. At any other time I would have been more than delighted to hear Cherry's zingy voice in my ear, but with the possibility of up to half a dozen calls coming in from potentially helpful citizens, including Jim Gray, this wasn't the time I would have chosen for a long, chatty conversation — even though I had been looking forward to long, chatty conversations with Cherry Dayne.

Thinking about that I was maybe just a little abrupt. "Frankly, I'm waiting for a bunch of calls, Cherry. I've been on the front-room phone for about half an hour, and some of the people may call back."

"Oh, that's right. This is your special phone. I forgot."

"Not so special. It's just — "

"I won't keep you, Shell. I thought of something to tell you. Say, why don't I come over? Or would you rather — "

"Of course, Cherry. I'd love to have you come over. I've been scheming how to get you into my bachelor's apartment. But — "

"I shouldn't have said that, should I? The man's supposed to do the asking. You must think I'm awful."

"I told you this morning I thought you were magnificent, 'then and now,' I believe I said, if memory fails to fail me. So add another now to it."

"Then and now-now? It sounds like those tribes in Africa — "

"Cherry — "

"I'm sorry. I'm cluttering up your phone, aren't I?"

"Not clut — "

"I'll come over. Is it all right?"

"Sure. Only if you've got something to tell me, you can tell me on the phone. After all, we've already been on it for — "

"You don't want me to come over."

I could feel my hand tightening around the receiver as if it were a deadly mamba — which is a very poisonous African snake — and I had to throttle it before it made me very poisoned. Women, and their yak-yak-yak, I thought. But, ah, I thought, when they stop yakking . . .

"Cherry," I said, "come over here this instant, you hear?"

"I will. I just remembered something else about that man I saw this morning. But I'd rather come over and tell you, anyway. Maybe you'll give me a drink."

"I'll ice the champagne. Or at least cool the gin. But — "

"Bye."

"Hang on a minute. Before you . . . Cherry?"

She'd hung up.

I had wanted to tell her she shouldn't go charging around pell-mell, flinging caution to the winds. There was still a guy who — by now — might know who it was that had spotted him at Slade's location this morning. In fact, the guy she'd just been talking about, I guessed.

I clunked the phone down on the receiver, but before I got out of the bedroom it rang. However, it wasn't Cherry calling back to tell me I hadn't said good-bye, but an old retired box man passing on some info he'd picked up. It was about another matter, though, and had nothing to do with the case.

When I hung up after a fast, rational dialogue, Cherry was even more on my mind. I could feel a lump of worry growing. I used the living-room phone to call her number, but there wasn't any answer. Apparently she was already on her way. Maybe I was being an old maid; probably there was nothing to worry about. Besides, her hotel was only a few blocks from here.

The bedroom phone rang again. Zip, bounce, second ring. It was Jim Gray.

"Yeah, Jim. Something?"

"Not much. But it could be in line with what you were talking about. This actress dame got pooped by a guy using a rifle, right? Right. Well, somebody brung in a out-of-town dropper for some kind of job. Got in just this morning. Expert with the little pieces but also a top man with the big heat. All I know is his name's Pete."

"Good work, Jim. I'll be in touch. Anything else?"

"That's it."

"You know what he looks like? Or who brought him in?"

"Nothin' about him — I was lucky to get this. Didn't dig it out, just happened to hear somebody mention seeing him get off a bus."

"Bus from where, you know?"

"Nope. And, man, I wasn't going to ask the guy I heard talking about it, neither. Not even for a bonus. It'd be what you call posthumorous."

"You get the bonus anyway. No more about Gant, huh?"

"Nothin'."

"I'm getting more and more interested in finding out if there's any connection betweeen Al and Jeremy Slade."

"Couldn't prove it by me one way or another. But here's something. If you could get a squeeze on Mooneyes somehow, get him to talking, he could probably tell you — that and a slew more."

"Mooneyes? That dim-brained — "

"Yeah. He's a dummy, all right. But he *always* drives the boys' heaps, and what he don't hear you wouldn't want ears for anyways. He just soaks it up. Goes without saying he wouldn't spill nothing about Al unless you had him by the fly with a eighty-pound vise, but might be that some time he'd fill you in on the other guys if approached proper. I just pass that on for free, Scott." He paused. "Actually, that is the cutest damn little radio-TV I ever did see."

I grinned. "Glad you like it, Jim."

The phone is right by my bed, and in the wall behind the headboard, toward the side next to the street, is a window I usually keep open. Sitting on the bed's edge, as I was then, I can look out the window on an angle toward North Rossmore, which runs in front of the Spartan.

So I spotted Cherry's pale blue Corvette Sting Ray when she slowed near the Spartan then swung in toward the curb, as her car passed out of my sight.

But then I saw something else, and between one second and the next my throat got dry. It was another car behind her. Nothing funny about the car itself. But whoever was driving doused his lights and angled in to the curb. He turned off the lights — while still out in the street — and *then* swung in to park.

Which is doing it backwards. Unless maybe you're worried about being spotted and move in too big a hurry.

"Thanks, Jim," I said quietly. "I'll see you." And hung up.

The car was just inside my line of vision, about half a block down the street. A dark sedan — it looked like a black Imperial. Nobody had gotten out of it yet. Cherry would be walking toward the Spartan now.

I moved to the window, eased the .38 from my holster, and leveled it at the car, just in case. But nothing happened. Nobody got out. I didn't notice any movement.

A few seconds passed. A man got out of the car on the right side — not the driver's side — and then walked across the street. If he'd been in the driver's seat he almost surely would have come out that side. So probably two guys had arrived in the car. Whoever they were.

The man stepped quickly across Rossmore and continued on his way, toward the Spartan. My door chimes rang. Cherry.

I started to pull back from the window when the man left the sidewalk, moved quickly into the near-darkness alongside the building.

That did it.

He was walking toward the door at the rear of the building.

I couldn't think of any good reason why he'd want to come in that way, to avoid going through the lobby and past the desk. But I could think of a couple of bad reasons.

I might feel silly if he turned out to be just the tenant three doors down the hall, coming in the back way because he felt like it. But I don't mind feeling silly from time to time in this life when death might be the alternative. Death for me, or for somebody else. Besides, I had that feeling. The tightness at the back of my neck, the small spot of coldness in my gut, the kind of electric tension over every inch of my skin. If that guy was the tenant three doors down the hall, every cell in my body was a liar.

The chimes bonged again.

I ran to the door, stood to one side — gun in hand — and yanked it open. It was Cherry, all right. I put the gun away quickly, but not before she saw it. I didn't even give her time to squeak, grabbed her arm and yanked her inside, slammed the door.

She opened her mouth — her big blue eyes were already the biggest I'd ever seen them — but I stopped her before she started.

"Be quiet, Cherry. This may be a false alarm, but — " There wasn't time for explanations. I said, "Just do what I tell you. There's an open window in the bedroom." I pointed. "Stand next to it. Somebody *may* come to this door, right behind you. If so, there might be some noise — noise, hell. I mean shooting. If there is, and I call to you, just stay where you are. But if I don't call, drop from the bedroom window and run. You got that?"

Something in my voice — or maybe the way I must have looked — got to her. She knew I wasn't playing games, this wasn't a gag, I was dead serious. She nodded, then said in a whisper, "If there's — noise, and you call, stay there. If not, go out the window."

If the man was coming here, he'd just about be starting up the stairs now. Twenty seconds, maybe twice that, depending on how fast he moved.

"One more thing," I said. "And this is important. *Don't* run toward the street. If this is anything at all, there's probably another man on Rossmore in a parked car — one that parked right after you did. *Don't* go that way. Run — and I mean run — away from the street and alongside the building. Get to a house, hotel, anything, and make a lot of noise. Get off the street and call the cops."

She nodded. "Yes. I can do it." She nodded again, nervously. She was pale. "But . . . what if you don't call. What — will that mean, Shell?"

My nerves don't usually climb out of my skin and squirm around, but for a second or two there they seemed to. Maybe it was the way she said it, and the sudden thought of what it would mean — the kind of thing you should never, never think about at a time like this. Or maybe it was the memory, too fresh because so recent, of the way the big boy died.

I said, "It'll mean you better run like hell."

I gave her a shove toward the bedroom, stepped to the wall next to the door, and pulled out the .38 again. Mentally, I was swearing. Swearing because Cherry was here; because if there was gunplay, even if I didn't get killed, I'd sure as hell have to kill the other guy — and I didn't want dead ones, I wanted them alive. I'd wanted the Collector alive. But you have to take what you get.

Damn it, I thought. If Cherry hadn't been here I might at least have dropped out the bedroom window, then tried to run around and come up behind the guy. This way we were just going to have to stand here two feet apart and let it happen.

The thoughts had been racing through my mind like a succession of moving pictures, among them the imaginary sight of me dropping from the window, falling the few feet to the ground.

But that one came back, not moving for some reason, but still like a snapshot. A snapshot of me suspended in the air.

And I thought of that ox.

I moved.

It wasn't a chain of thought, not a logical progression from A to B to C, it was all just suddenly there — beginning, middle, and end.

Six feet away was the big heavy leather chair I like to lounge in. I jumped to it, spun it across the carpet, and placed it four feet from the door, its back toward the door but slanting into the room.

Then I ran to the bedroom. I'd figured I had twenty, maybe forty seconds. How much time had passed since then I hadn't any idea. Maybe twenty seconds; maybe fifty. Most of it had been passed just thinking, and you can't measure thought in seconds or split-seconds, not in normal time. But I knew it was time now. It was time.

I grabbed the big mirror leaning against the bedroom wall, rushed back, and propped it against the chair, as straight up and down as I could get it. Pressed against the wall next to the front door and looking into the mirror I could see the door itself, smack on. Not my reflection, but the door. When the door opened, I would see him — whoever he was — and he would see me. Or, rather that big-ox reflection of me.

I'd been too busy concentrating on the job at hand to pay attention to anything else. But now, with a sensation like cold water pouring down the inside of my spine, I saw Cherry, still standing in the middle of the room. She had been watching everything I did, probably as wide-eyed as she still was, rigid, as if nailed to the floor.

I took a step toward her — and the chimes rang.

I felt the first soft lick of weakness then, at the back of my knees. After long-continued tension, or sudden and extreme emotion, that weakness comes. For a little while. It passes. But it had come too soon. Everything was falling apart, going to hell. And Cherry was right in the middle of it, right in the way.

I moved fast to Cherry, sliding my feet on the carpet.

"Get out of here!" I said softly, but it sounded like a distant yell. "You want to get killed?"

She snapped out of it. But she hadn't moved yet.

The seconds were dying. Too many seconds. I turned my head toward the door and called, "Yeah, yo! That you, Paul?" I guess that's what I said; I'm not too damn sure what I did say.

Then I put my face about two inches from Cherry's and hissed, *"Cherry, get into the bedroom!"*

Her eyes were dark with something like panic. She looked as if she were going to faint. Her mouth was stretched wide and the corners were jumping up and down, twitching like rattled Jell-O.

I thought she was passing out on me. But then I got it — and she won me right there. I don't give a damn if she was acting like a maniac, or if there were eight guys with bombs and machine guns at the door. She was trying to smile.

And just a beat, half a second after I'd hissed, *"Cherry get into the bedroom!"*, she said, with her lips quivering, eyes like saucers, "Shell — " gulp — "I thought you'd *never* ask me."

Then she turned with real speed and moved, ghostlike, over the floor. Into the bedroom. By then I was thumping toward the door. "Hey, yo!" I called — or something. "Just a second, Paul."

The last two steps were like the earlier ones, shoes sliding on the carpet. But I moved fast. Pressed against the wall, gun in my right hand — down at my side, not held in front of me — I used my left hand to turn the doorknob. Not too fast. Just like a dumb cluck opening the door for old Paul.

Then I gave the knob a flip and yanked my left hand back, looking straight into the mirror.

The door swung open.

Seventeen

He was a pro. And better than most.

So much better I don't think I would have beaten him. I honestly think he'd have killed me.

I had a gun; I was ready, sure. But before I could have pulled the trigger I would have had to be certain. Not guessing. Certain it wasn't *really* Paul — or at least that it was a man with a gun, not just a man.

But not this bastard.

He was here on a job, a killing job. Or, rather, a double killing job, considering the rest of it. And all he had to do was see a body and put a bullet into it.

The door was only part way open, still moving. I could see half of him. Which meant he could see only half of me. But that was when he fired. Right through the wood, before the door was even out of the way.

The explosion sounded like a stick of dynamite going off. It was like a fist slamming my ear. The door jerked as the slug tore through it, and mingled with that crack and sound of wood splintering was the tinkling crash of shattering glass. Right in the middle of it his gun blasted again. No wait, no hesitation. The old murder one-two; if the first slug didn't do the job, the second would. And then maybe a few more in the head. The double rule of the sonsofbitches: Don't take any chances — and don't give him a chance.

The gunshots echoed, and burnt powder was sharp in my nostrils. The whole thing filled less than a second. Then, in sudden quiet, a piece of glass fell with a tinkle. He was halfway into the room by then, his gun held before him but his face already starting to show the shock — and beginnings of fear.

I didn't have to step forward. All I had to do was turn left a little and move my back away from the wall. Then I rammed my Colt into his side. Just in and out; you don't leave your gun touching a cutie like this one, you don't give him a chance at it.

So, in and then out as I took a step backward, away from him. But when I rammed the gun into him I got a lot of me behind it, and there's two hundred and six pounds if I use it all. Maybe I didn't break the rib, but I bent it, and a sound like *chuh* was squeezed out of his mouth.

I held the gun on him, hammer thumbed back, and said, "You want it?"

His gun hand jerked. But just a little. Hardly enough to notice. That was all. He didn't want it.

I had spoken so softly that, normally, he might not have heard me at all. If you didn't know it before, you'd know it at a time like this: We move through our days only half alive, our senses dulled, a film before our eyes and plugs in our ears. But at such times all the senses become abnormally acute, everything is brighter, louder, more vivid. And sweeter — all of life becomes very sweet. Maybe it's nature's way of giving an extra chance to a man when he's next door to dying; it seems a hell of a note, though, that most of us have to get killed, or damn near killed, to find out about it.

Anyway, this boy heard me.

And he heard me when I half whispered, "That heat of yours is cocked, friend, so don't drop it."

He didn't. He leaned forward, very slowly. Sweat glistened on his upper lip. He did it right, slow-motion and easy, never letting the gun barrel stray toward me. He placed the gun on the floor like a mother patting a baby, then straightened up. A long sigh spilled from his lips as he came erect again.

"Kick it," I said. "Straight in."

He put his foot next to the gun, shoved it over the carpet.

I said, "Now, come on in, Pete."

He stepped farther into the room, and I slammed the door, then called out, "It's O.K., Cherry. Just stay put."

For all I knew, she was out that window and tearing down a street somewhere. But right now there were other things to take care of, two other things.

I said, "Look over there, Pete," and pointed to the far wall. He turned that way, his back to me. I got his gun, the almost-standard piece of the hood and heavy man, a Colt .45 automatic pistol.

I took out the slip and ejected the cartridge in the gun's chamber, then slapped the bare clip back in the Colt's heavy butt. "It is Pete, isn't it?" I asked him conversationally.

He didn't say anything.

Well, if he wouldn't join in the conversation, there was no sense keeping him here. Holding the Colt's barrel in my right hand, I swung it briskly through the air and cracked that heavy butt on the back of his skull, and Pete was no longer here.

I went out of the apartment and down the hall toward the back stairs, to take care of the other thing.

It was dark alongside the Spartan's wall, but street lights dimly illuminated Rossmore, straight ahead. Gun in my right hand, I walked toward the street, reversing the path that Pete — or whoever he was — had taken on his way to my door. Even though I hadn't actually seen anybody else in the black Imperial, I would have given ten to one a man was now sitting at the wheel, waiting to celebrate with his buddy. And I would have given nearly as good odds it was Joe "Mooneyes" Garella.

I remembered what Jim Gray had said to me, only minutes ago. If I could "squeeze" Mooneyes somehow, he would tell me much I wanted to know and a lot I wasn't even curious about. That trigger-quick dropper was sprawled on my apartment floor, and in another minute or two I might have all I needed to squeeze the juice out of Mooneyes. It seemed too good to be true.

It was.

I goofed.

I knew that if there was a man in the car he would have heard the shots — the whole neighborhood would have; heads had been hanging out of suddenly opened doors in the hallway as I'd left the building. I knew he'd be expecting his chum to come running back the way he'd come — that was why I'd come this way instead of trying to sneak up on the man from behind, which probably wouldn't have worked either. I was going to be Shell Scott's killer, not Shell Scott, and with luck I might hop right inside that Imperial before the guy in it knew what was happening.

But you can't think of everything; at least, I can't, and I forgot one rather obvious thing: Shell Scott's killer didn't have a big gob of white hair.

At least, I guess that was it. When I started angling across the street toward the Imperial, my head must have looked like an albino bat flying at him. He naturally had the engine idling, and he just slapped the car into gear and gave it the gas.

He was moving toward me before he switched on the lights, and when they poured over me I had already heard the sudden roar of the engine and was trying to slow down, to change direction.

There wasn't time.

He was right on me, practically on top of me. He was dead center, too, big chromed bumper straight ahead and headlights to my left and right. And it had happened so suddenly I was still running forward; there wasn't a chance I could jump to one side or the other, not a chance in hell.

I didn't think out the next move, it just happened. I was as surprised as he must have been. I gave a great, an enormous bound — forward, as if I were trying to reach my bedroom phone in one jump instead of four, spread out in the air as though planning to fly smack through the windshield, arms stretched out as if to grab him. If he really had thought at first that a monster bat was going for him, now he must have thought it had turned back into Dracula — because in that split-second I actually saw his hands leave the wheel and go up to shield his eyes.

You've seen these highly athletic fellows leap gracefully at leather horses in gymnasiums, and sort of pat them with their outstretched hands as they go over, and then do a flip in the air and land past the horse, sort of dancing on their feet? Well, I guess that's what I thought I was doing.

I'm not sure what I thought, because I wasn't thinking. There are times when a man must stop depending on his brain and use something else, and I was probably figuring this problem out with my tail. Even though I was doing it, even though I was in the air and turning damn near upside down, very nicely, and the car's driver was going "Aacck" and nipping his hands over his enormous pale eyes — yeah, it was Mooneyes — to protect them from the gruesome sight, I had no high hopes for a successful culmination to this maneuver.

As I say, you've seen these athletic fellows leaping over horses. Well, I am not one of them. I've got lots of muscles, but I'm not Nijinsky. Even though this movement had been engineered by my subconscious mind — I wouldn't have done anything like this if I'd been conscious — it would have been a catastrophe if Mooneyes hadn't helped me.

Yes, he helped me.

He didn't mean to. He fully intended to run me down, and squash me, and maybe then back up over me a couple of times. But that was when *he* had been the attacker.

Now, the bat man was attacking *him*.

What could he do?

He defended himself, naturally.

He slammed on the brakes so fast he must have sprained the sole of his foot. It didn't help much. But it helped a little. The tires squealed on the asphalt as my hands touched the hood of his car, and at that point, even if not using any brain, I used all the brawn there was in those arms and shoved like a man pushing death away, which is what I was doing.

I turned completely over in the air, feet flying over my head — and onto the roof of the Imperial. Not like Nijinsky. Not like those athletic fellows. Like a sack of cement. But instead of being rammed head-on by the Imperial's front end and chromed bumper I landed tail-on atop the Imperial's roof. I landed and bounced and skidded, then I was going one way in the air and the Imperial was going the opposite way beneath me.

Then I landed on the street. It seemed as though I landed simultaneously on both shoulders, my fanny, and my head, though there must have been some lapse of time between separate impacts. But I managed to land at one time or another on most of my anatomy, and it didn't do any of it much good.

I was alive, though. Bruised, aching, the skin scraped from one hand and my right ear, muscles pulled in my thigh, and a large ache in my — well, delicately, my derrière.

All that — and happy.

Mooneyes didn't even try to back up and run over me. He knew when he'd had enough. There is a time for fight and a time for flight, and he'd had enough fighting for tonight.

I sat in the middle of the street for a while, because I needed time. Time to become capable of getting up. I made it on the second try. Then I found my gun. Then I limped back up to my apartment.

It was a good thing I hadn't sat down there in the street any longer. The guy on the floor was twitching a little, coming back. Glass was all over, every which way. It figured. There went my damned do-it-yourself project, already — I told you.

Cherry wasn't in sight.

I hobbled into the bedroom.

She was there, standing by the window, but with her back to it.

"Cherry, it's O.K. You can come out in the front room and join us now."

She fainted.

Caught me by surprise. Fooled me. Like I said, you can't think of everything. Probably this was going to take some time, so I went back and, once more, hit what I now thought of as the back of Pete's head. Maybe he wasn't Pete. No matter; whoever he was, he stopped twitching.

And I started. It didn't last long. It never does. And it wasn't fun while it lasted. But, then, this wasn't a fun night. I found some brandy and had a shot, then poured a couple fingers into another wineglass and took it into the bedroom.

Cherry was still crumpled on the floor. I picked her up and put her on the bed. It wasn't easy.

Then I looked at her. Gorgeous. Absolutely gorgeous. Gorgeous Cherry on my bed. At last. Me standing there. Brandy in wineglasses. Room not completely dark, just dim, almost like candlelight. That's the way to live, huh?

I looked at myself in the cracked mirror. Yeah, I'd ruined some more of my wardrobe. And some more of me.

Cherry moved, sighed.

I sat down on the edge of the bed next to her.

When her eyes fluttered open I said, "Hi. Relax. How about a drink?"

"What?"

"This'll spark you up. Here's some brandy." I was casual about it. So I'd saved her life probably. And mine. And captured a vicious killer. No sense pouring it on. Play it light, I figured.

She didn't say anything right away. She sat up, blinked a few times, and took a deep breath. Then she looked up at me, and her face softened. I wasn't sure, but I thought her lips curved just a little into a small smile.

"But, Shell," she said, "I don't *like* brandy."

Eighteen

Actually, she did — that *had* been a small smile I'd detected. She even had a second brandy after that first one. There was more to this gal than met the eye — and one hell of a lot met the eye.

I said, "Want another brandy, Cherry? Hey — that's good; if only it was cherry brandy — "

"It's awful."

"Yeah, I suppose it was. But I hurt my head."

"You poor thing."

"Sympathy. That's what I like. Tender solicitude — "

"Oh, stop it. You're alive — "

The lightness suddenly got heavy. Her voice broke. Her shoulders rose and fell, and then she pressed her hands to her face and started sobbing, sobbing and making small shrieking sounds, muffled against her palms.

I put my arms around her, pulled her against me. After a while she stopped crying and lifted her head. Tears glistened on her cheeks, and mascara had made shadows beneath her eyes.

"Oh, Shell," she said in a new, a different voice. "I heard the shots, and waited. You didn't call. It seemed forever. I was so afraid. . . . I thought — "

Her mouth was only inches from mine. And then an inch, and then . . .

I had known kissing Cherry would almost surely be lots of fun. I hadn't guessed it would be whatever it is that starts where fun leaves off. How can a kiss be — or at least seem to be — so much? So much more than just lips meeting? Man, I don't know. I guess it's that sometimes, once in a while and rarely, rarely, lips connect in a way that disconnects a man's noodle and sends it into an nth dimension.

Something like that must have happened.

Something like that . . .

They were lips that said hello and were warm friends two seconds later, carrying on a conversation Casanova would have censored, carrying on a dialogue to bring dead libidoes back from limbo, carrying on a bedroomy hoo-hah in hot, hushed whispers — man, how they carried on. It wasn't a kiss; it was lips making love between clean sheets illumined by candlelight. It was the scent of sex, the sound of blood, soft light behind closed lids, the taste of mouth and lips and tears and tongue. And maybe heart. It was all the five senses, a whole census of senses. . . . That nth dimension, I guess. If there's a better name, it's not important. But it lasted half of forever, and ended as soon as it started.

There were whispered words, and then Cherry pulled it up again, up into lightness. Where, after all, it has to be most of the time.

"Well," she said, "now you know why I don't drink much brandy."

"I have gin and vermouth. Which would you like?"

"They might even be good together. Mostly gin?"

"I'm afraid there isn't time to experiment — even with something as good as that might be. But . . . There's a guy in the front room."

"Is he — "

"Not dead. Unconscious, as the result of a splitting headache."

I stood up, but as she got off the bed Cherry said, "Shell, I saw what happened — in the street, I mean. I was looking out the window. I thought you were going to get killed."

"I considered that possibility myself. Actually, that's all I considered."

"You're — a remarkable man," she said quietly.

I didn't quite know what to say to that. So I mumbled, "Oh, I'm just naturally graceful," and then we were walking into the front room, and Cherry said:

"Eek."

I'd told her there was a guy out here. But I guess she hadn't expected to see glass all over, and blood on the back of the man's head — there's usually blood when you hit a man as hard as I'd hit him twice. Besides, talking about it is one thing, and seeing it is another.

"It's . . . it's not like in a movie, is it?" she said.

"Nope. But we have our monsters, too." I stepped to the unconscious man and rolled him over onto his back.

Cherry's gasp told me all I wanted to know. But she said it anyway. "That's the man I saw this morning."

"Yeah, well he saw you, too, and hunted you down. To your hotel, obviously. I know he wanted to get both of us, but I'm surprised he didn't try for you there."

"I was in a hurry," she said, "so I had a bellboy get my car from the hotel lot and bring it around front. Maybe — "

"Almost surely. He must have been watching for you to show in the lot. Incidentally, what was it you wanted to tell me about the guy?"

"Oh, I remembered that, after he stared at me this morning, when he turned around to get into his car, I saw a patch or bandage, something on the back of his neck. It stuck up over his shirt collar." She smiled slightly. "I guess it wasn't very important, but you told me to tell you if I thought of *anything*."

I rolled the guy on his side and took a look. There was a dirty bandage on his neck, all right. The bum had boils. Which wasn't surprising. Most hoods are sick, mentally *and* physically, and sour blood is merely one of the hoodlum's ills. Most of the something-for-nothing creeps — in or out of the underworld — are filled with hate and resentment directed toward somebody or everybody, and health can't bloom with those poisons in the blood.

"It's not very important now, is it?" Cherry said.

"Maybe not now. But it *could* have been plenty important. It could have helped me tag the guy."

Sirens again.

I sighed. After that kiss, I had momentarily entertained the thought of a quiet evening here at home — with Cherry, and gin-and-vermouth, soft music from the stereo, and all that. But it wouldn't work. Not after last night, and this morning, and the Collector, and now the guy on the floor. I'd be spending the rest of this evening with the police.

My batting average was pretty good tonight. I was right about that, too.

I got started early the next morning, despite the fact that a long session with the police cut my sleeping time down to three hours. Even with an early start, it was ten A.M. before I picked up any more information worth hanging on to.

I'd learned that the Anglo-Western Bank on Vermont had supplied Slade with the bulk of the financing for his previous *Goo* movies, and the man who had approved previous loans was a vice president named Brown. I was in Brown's office, seated opposite him before his desk, a few minutes before ten A.M.

Before coming here I had checked the files of local newspapers and pinned down the time of Vivyan Virgin's absence from the *Ghost of the Creeping Goo* set. So after the preliminary conversation I said, "Mr. Brown, I understand Mr. Slade was pretty hard up for money during filming of his previous picture, but did manage to complete the film. Did he get an extension of, or addition to, his loan from this bank? That would have been about nine months ago, when one of the principal actresses was unable to work on the film. She was out for two or three weeks, I understand."

"Yes," he nodded. "Miss Virgin. I recall the situation quite well. Mr. Slade spoke to me at that time, requesting an additional loan."

"He did, huh? Did he get it?"

"He did not."

Bankers aren't in the habit of cutting up their customers, or even saying much about their financial status. But by listening between the lines, so to speak, it became clear enough to me that Mr. Brown had considered Slade not only a poor risk but desperate for money. The most obvious thing he said was, "It seemed to me, at that point, it would merely be throwing good money after bad. So I did not approve the loan."

"He definitely did need more money, though, didn't he? To finish his film?"

"That is the impression I received."

"Well, if he didn't get it from you, where did he get it?"

He smiled. "I have no idea."

That was good enough for me. I thanked Mr. Brown and left.

For the next twenty minutes I didn't do anything. That is, not anything active. I just stayed parked in the bank's lot and sat there thinking. I got out my notebook and pen, listed everything I knew for sure about the case, plus most of what I'd guessed, looked it over, thought about it some more.

Before the twenty minutes was up I'd decided on two courses of action. One of them I could have found and followed before; it was glaringly apparent now. The other was, perhaps, one I shouldn't ever have thought of at all.

The easy one had to do with that piece of paper I'd picked up outside Pike's home, night before last. I'd read it over half a dozen times without getting a clue as to who had written it, but now, as if the time was finally right, I realized I'd been going at the problem backwards.

There wasn't a clue to the letter writer's identity in the page of the letter itself, true enough; but there was a lead to somebody else. And from that somebody else I might be able to discover who'd written the letter — if I could find him.

I'd been carrying the sheet of paper around with me and now I got it out and read it again. Yeah, there it was, the last thing on the page: "... of course I kept the money for the abortion. But I never had no idea when I went for help — help! ha-ha! — to Dr. Willim — "

Dr. Willim. There were so many misspellings in the rest of the page that possibly the name should have been William, or Wallace, or even George. But it was the only lead I had.

Even without that I had almost enough. I was pretty sure I knew the big answers, and some of the small ones; but to wrap it up I needed more information. I knew where I could probably get it, and there was — maybe — a way to get it; but it would take some doing. In fact, I could get killed. And judging by the two narrow squeaks I'd already had, I thought unhappily, I should be about due.

Besides, it was a kind of goofy idea to begin with, and I wasn't sure I could set it up. But *if* I could . . .

I used a pay phone booth outside the bank. Three dimes and another twenty minutes later I hung up, smiling. Setting it up hadn't been so tough after all — just horribly expensive. This was going to cost me close to a couple of thousand bucks, maybe more. From twenty to forty out-of-work actors and actresses at fifty bucks apiece, plus five more who would have speaking and/or acting parts for a total of another eight hundred clams.

Plus the dime I'd spent to call Ed Howell.

He was going to handle this part for me, and set it up if he could. I knew he wasn't required on the set of Slade's picture today — they were shooting the queen's execution and some scenes with Gruzakk and Cherry Dayne — and he'd told me a couple of the other principals and several bit players were free, too, and he'd try to get some of them as well.

In addition to the initial expense, if anything went wrong there would undoubtedly be lots and lots of fines, and some of us might even wind up in jail. Certainly *I* would.

But it was either that or torture — that is, trying to beat the truth out of the guy. And I've never been able to pound on a man to make him talk, or break his bones, or burn out his eyes; that sort of thing doesn't appeal to me. Perhaps because the beater inevitably suffers more lasting damage than does the beaten. Not to mention the mere practical angle: After suffering enough pain some men will spill almost anything, and there's no guarantee it's the truth.

No, torture was out. At least, physical torture. A little psychological sweating, though — I'll go along with that. Now all I had to do was grab Mooneyes and somehow get him to go where I wanted him to go. That part I hadn't figured out yet.

In the meantime, there was the other project, the "Dr. Willim" angle. While still in the booth I turned to the yellow pages, found "Physicians and Surgeons, M.D." There were a couple of Williams with an "s" but no Willim. So I checked them one at a time. It took a while — down to "M." But there it was: Dr. Macey. Dr. Willim Macey. She'd spelled it right after all. He was a psychoanalyst, with an address on Rodeo Drive in Beverly Hills.

And that, of course, tied it up with a pink ribbon.

Dr. Macey's office was small, but expensively furnished, and it was certainly in the high-rent district. I think they lease Rodeo Drive by the carat rather than front foot. I walked over soft gray carpeting to a desk behind which sat a middle-aged lady with bags under her eyes and told her I'd like to see Dr. Macey.

Oh, I couldn't do that, she informed me. My goodness, no. I gathered I should have applied for an appointment about five to seven years ago. So I asked the lady for an envelope, sealed my crumpled letter-page in it, and told her that, if she'd give it to Dr. Macey, he would see me.

She gave me a look indicating her belief that I probably needed to see Dr. Macey very, very badly, but she took my unorthodox note in to him, anyway.

It was like magic.

She came out. Half a minute later a young, shapely, well-dressed — and angry — woman came out. She stopped, wheeled, looked back into the doctor's inner office and cried, "I've never been so — I just *got* here. How *could* you?"

In the doorway appeared a tall, slightly fat, pleasant looking man wearing chin whiskers and horn-rimmed glasses.

"I'm sorry, Mrs. Mills," he said. "It's unavoidable, I assure you. There will, of course, be no . . ." His eyes fell on me then, and he blinked, as if startled. He'd been expecting somebody else, maybe? After a pause and another blink or two he continued, "No charge for today's — "

"I should *hope* not." She stormed out, slamming the door.

I stood up.

Dr. Macey started to say something to me, then shrugged and went back into his office. I followed him, closing the door behind me.

He walked to his couch — a real couch, low, dark leather, well worn — and sat on its edge. He reached into his coat pocket and pulled out the envelope and sheet of paper I'd sent him. They were crumpled into a wad.

"I thought I was through with you," he said, not looking at me.

I didn't say anything, let him carry the ball.

"I've given you everything I could." He looked at me then and blinked, blinked again. "You don't look like — "

Now that the initial shock had lessened somewhat he was pulling himself together. Maybe even getting a bit suspicious of me. So I said quickly, "You mean the other guy? The big slob, baldy with the big feet?"

There wasn't any large reaction; he just said, "Yes. What are you doing, passing me around?"

"He couldn't come this time. He got himself killed yesterday."

"That's too bad," he said, as if delighted with the news. "I thought I was finished with . . . with all of this." He moved the crumpled papers in his hand.

"You're never finished with blackmail, doctor."

At the word he winced, blinked some more, then said, "I suppose not." His eyes strayed toward his desk.

Analysts sometimes record the freewheeling ramblings and free associations of their patients so that later, at their leisure, they can pore over every word, nuance, and inflection, seeking something that can be crammed into the Freudian mold.

So I said, "Turn off the bug."

"Bug?" He blinked. "Oh, the recorder. Of course." He scowled, but went over to his desk, opened a drawer and pushed a button, then sat down behind his desk. "Well, what do you want this time?"

"The same as before."

Yeah, he was suspicious, all right. "That's not good enough," he said. "What do you want?"

I said, "Information. You didn't give the other guy any money, did you?" Then I let myself get suspicious and said, suspiciously, "Or *did* you?"

That really got a lot of blinks out of him. "You know damn well I didn't pay that paranoid brute with mon — " He stopped. "Who are you?" he said after a pause. "Where did you get Jerrilee's letter?" I grinned.

"Who are you?" he said again. "Haven't I seen you — "

I had a hunch I might not get much more out of Dr. Willim Macey. No matter; he'd already told me most of what I'd been after. I knew Jerrilee had written the letter, and that he'd paid, but probably hadn't paid with money. I could have walked in and told him my name, that I was a private detective and so on. But men being blackmailed couldn't be blackmailed in the first place if they would talk about their trouble to policemen or even to private detectives. Almost surely he would have told me to go fly a kite.

It was reasonably certain he would put two and two together soon anyway. My picture had been in the local papers often enough that he'd probably seen it at one time or another. Besides — I like to think — I don't *look* like a crook.

But I tried one more shot. "You paid off with dope from your files, didn't you, doctor? Records, transcripts of recordings, that sort of material?"

He didn't answer for a long time. Finally he said, "I'm not going to tell you a damn thing. I'm . . . going to call the police."

He put his hand on his desk phone. I waited. A man with nothing to hide would call the law, all right. "Go ahead," I said.

He didn't call. "I insist you tell me who you are," he said.

"I'm Shell Scott, Dr. Macey. I'm a private detective. In the interests of my client, I've been — "

He didn't let me finish. He was swearing at me. Then he said, "A private detective!" as if that were something much, much worse than an Oedipus complex. "I *will* call the police!" He was dialing this time, going through with it. He wasn't afraid of a private detective. "I'll have you arrested. You'll lose your license."

"What'll you tell them, doctor?" I asked him.

"That you tried to blackmail — "

"Wrong, doctor. Wrong again."

He stared at me, phone against his ear.

I said, "I have *not* attempted to blackmail you. I've asked nothing of you except information. I didn't tell you my name, true, but you simply assumed I was another guy here to bleed you, right? I'm merely an investigator, doing a little investigating."

He thought about it.

Then I said, "Besides, you don't want them to know about Jerrilee, do you?"

He looked left, right, up, and down, blinking about three times a second. No, he didn't want them to know about Jerrilee. He hung up the phone.

"Now," I said, "if you'll just level with me, there's a good chance I can be of help to you."

"Get out of here."

That's the way it went. I kept trying, but Dr. Macey was going to have nothing more to do with me. And he sure wasn't going to tell me anything — at least, not anything more.

I stood up, leaned over the desk, and reached for the papers still in his hand. "I'll take that," I said.

Sometimes the confident, self-assured approach works. Not this time. He shoved his chair back and got to his feet, the papers balled in his right hand. "You'll have to fight me for it," he said.

Well. He had more spunk than I'd guessed. Or else he was frightened half to death. I said, "Keep it, then. I don't want it any more." I straightened up. "Look, Dr. Macey, you're understandably upset. But, believe me, I can probably help get these people off your back. If you'll tell me the truth about — "

"I'll tell you nothing." He was pale, but with spots of color in his cheeks.

"Let me tell you, then," I said. "The girl who wrote the letter, of which you're now clutching one page — Jerrilee — was either a patient of yours or a playmate. No, a patient — she said she went to you for help. With exclamation points."

He swallowed, and seemed to become even more pale, but didn't speak. "She got in trouble," I went on, "to use the common euphemism. Right here on your couch, according to her testimony. Well, to make a long story short, you were approached for blackmail and hit with the info I've just been talking about, and probably a good deal more."

He stayed clammed up.

"So you paid," I said. "But not with money. The people running this operation didn't want money, not from you. You were a gold mine. From you they could get — and I'll give ten to one they got — very juicy info on some of the most important, and wealthiest, people in and around Hollywood and Beverly Hills. How am I doing?"

Judging by his expression I was doing fine, but he wasn't speaking to me.

"Among those people, about whom you innocently amassed a few tons of extremely personal information, some of it immensely damaging if it should become public knowledge, was an actress named Vivyan Virgin. She flipped out of a movie nine months ago and started undergoing analysis by Dr. Macey — by you. Six months ago, *after* she'd been spilling to you for three months, she was blackmailed undoubtedly with the info she'd been spilling. Your blackmailers took the info they'd squeezed from you and used it to blackmail her — and probably dozens of others."

I paused. "Well, doctor?"

He was trying to kill me with his eyes. "You're a liar," he said. "None of it's true. None of it. You're — " his eyes brightened a little — "*sick*. You're *sick*."

I shook my head. "I may be nuts, but I'm not sick — and I don't think I'm nuts, either." I turned toward the door, then stopped and tried one last time.

"You're making a mistake, doctor — another mistake. I'm not trying to ride you. I don't want to add to your troubles — just the opposite. If you'll cooperate with me, there's a damned good chance I can help you."

He was working himself into a kind of controlled frenzy. Arms flapping a little, eyes blinking like the dickens.

I went on, "I told you the truth when I said the other guy, that big greasy slob, got himself killed. What I didn't tell you was that I shot him. I'm on your side; I'm trying — "

Telling him I'd shot the Collector didn't help. I think it gave him an idea, instead. He yanked open a desk drawer, raked through it, slammed it, and opened the drawer below it.

My instant deduction was that he had a gun somewhere in that desk but just couldn't remember what drawer he'd last seen it in. I got out of there before he remembered.

Well, it was something I'd known for a long time. But it's hard not to fall into that old human error. Proof of which can be found by a glance at most social workers, do-gooders, and vote-hungry politicians. It's just no good trying to help people until they ask for help — or, at least, until they want it.

But at least I'd learned a little, and hadn't been shot — probably because Dr. Macey couldn't remember where his gun was.

Mooneyes, though, might be a different kettle of fish. He knew at all times where his gun was. He didn't go out with girls much — or vice versa — and he consequently lavished a lot of attention and loving care upon his heater. He had dates with it. And he carried it, appropriately for the object of such a long-lived romance, near to his heart.

He was pretty dumb; but he knew where his heart was. He didn't have to open any drawers to find it.

Yes, Mooneyes might be different.

Nineteen

It was nearly eleven-thirty A.M., and this early in the day it was difficult to say where Mooneyes would be. Later there was a good chance he — and Gant, plus another muscleman or three — would be holding court in the Apache. But that much later would be too much later.

I made a few calls trying to locate him, without success, then thought again of Annette.

Annette was one of the several dozen people I'd phoned in the last thirty-six hours or so, while putting my lines out. I'd called her before because I knew she'd gone out with Mooneyes once, a month or so ago; but she hadn't been able to give me any information I could use. Presumably she would if she could, since — I gathered — for practically anybody, one date with Mooneyes was enough, and a little more. She had told me, though, that Mooneyes was eager for number two, and kept calling her. So she might know where to reach him.

Annette was the second-featured performer at the Swank Theater on Spring Street — the gal "understeadying," as she put it, the artist who got top billing. Annette was a stripper; I had seen Annette's act; it was a safe bet Mooneyes liked Annette even better than his gun. It might work.

If it did, it would be handy, too. Another of those three dimes I'd spent earlier had been for a call to Ron Smith, a former court reporter who now worked in an office at the Hall of Justice, which was only a few blocks from the Swank. I knew Judge Croffer was presiding over a session of Superior Court in one of the Hall of Justice courtrooms, and Smith had agreed to let me know — if I called back — when the judge went to lunch. Despite crowded calendars, judges always adjourn court for lunch. Often for a couple of hours or so. But Judge

Croffer was probably getting hungry about now, which didn't give me much time.

So, without further delay I drove over to see Annette. She didn't go on until one P.M. — after the triple feature — but I figured she'd be backstage at the Swank. She was.

Because, as she explained it, Mooneyes gave her "creepy goose bumps," she was more than willing to cooperate with me in an attempt to put him out of circulation. I told her that, if this operation miscarried, Mooneyes might suspect her of fingering him, which could make things sticky for her, but that I'd do my best to keep that from happening and felt reasonably sure I could.

Annette wasn't worried. She could handle Mooneyes if it came to that. "Besides," she went on, "I won't even ask him to come over. I'll just say hello, and do a couple of bumps with my tonsils, and he'll ask if he can come watch my act. So I'll tell him I couldn't care less. And he'll come over."

Women, I thought, are the last practitioners of black and gray magic.

Anyway, just as Cherry had known how to reach me, Annette knew where to get in touch with Mooneyes; so with that part set I called the Hamilton Building and got Hazel, the cute little trick on the second-floor switchboard.

"Shell here, Hazel. Those two guys I phoned you about earlier show up?"

"Just a few minutes ago, Shell. My, they look rough. Who are they?"

"I'll tell you later — they're supposed to look rough. Send them over to the Swank Theater, will you?"

"Swank? Shell, I'm surprised at you — "

"No, you're not," I said, and hung up.

"O.K.," I said to Annette.

She called two numbers and got results at the second one. "Hi, Clarence," she said. "How are you, hon?"

She listened, looked at me and stuck out her tongue, grimacing, then put on a smile.

"Oh, Clarence; I've *told* you not to say things like that," she cooed in a tone that begged him to say things like that. "What? Just practicing a new number. Oh, no, Clarence, no, you shouldn't come over. But it's only a little — what?"

Annette looked at me and winked. It was practically set. I'm surprised there aren't more women detectives. They wouldn't even have to carry guns.

And then it filtered in that maybe we were working on the wrong case here. Clarence? Who in hell was Clarence?

"Psst," I said. "Annette — not Clarence. Mooneyes!"

She ignored me. "Well, if you *want* to, Clarence. But I'd realty rather you *didn't*. I haven't perfected the — the movement yet. What? Oh, you devil, you. Really? Well, I just wanted to talk to you, hon."

"Psst! Not Clarence."

"Now, you stop saying that," she cooed. "No, you'd better not come over — not until I've perfected the movement. Bye, Clarence."

"Psst!"

She'd hung up.

"There," she said to me. "He'll be here before you know it. And he'll never guess I wanted him to come."

"Who would?" I scowled. "The only trouble is, we were to use all that female fiendishness on Mooneyes."

"Silly, that *was* Mooneyes."

"Clarence? The Mooneyes I referred to is monickered Joe 'Mooneyes' Garella, and if there are two guys named Mooneyes — "

"Shell, will you *listen?* Joe isn't his real name. It's Clarence Garella. Hardly anybody knows his real name but me — he told me everything about himself. His dep . . . deprivation in childhood and all."

"He must've."

"And he didn't like the name Clarence, so when he was a kid he started calling himself Joe."

I nodded, feeling what was almost a kind of sadness. For a moment I felt quite sorry for Clarence Garella. Even though he'd undoubtedly picked up that "deprivation" bit from the prison psychologist or a social worker during his last stretch in stir, it was probably true that he'd had an unhappy childhood; and he sure was not having a very happy adulthood. It was, I suppose, a pity. But there was nothing to prevent him from turning in his Colt .45 for a pick and shovel if he felt like it. Oddly, he had never felt like it.

Besides, he'd shot several guys. Killed at least two or three. And he'd driven a professional killer up to the Spartan last night so the cold-eyed bastard could murder me. And Clarence must have known that if the pro got me he'd pump a couple of slugs into Cherry, too. More, Clarence had tried to run over me and squash me last night. I suppose it was a pity, but nonetheless I wasn't going to drown in it. I wasn't going to rehabilitate him. I was going to fix Mooneyes good, if I could.

I thanked Annette, wished her luck perfecting that movement, and walked down to Spring Street. The two men Hazel had sent over from my office were just parking in a lot across the street. At least I assumed they were the two, though we hadn't met. I bought three tickets from the gal in the Swank's box office, and waited.

They looked right. One was about my size, the other shorter but a good deal heavier. He looked like an ex-fullback. Both of them were dressed in dark suits and wore dark snap-brim hats.

They recognized me and joined me on the sidewalk. I made sure they were my men — the taller one was Gill, the ex-fullback was Tony — then led them off the street into the theater's lobby.

"You know what you're supposed to do?" I asked them.

The taller of the two nodded. "Roughly," he said. "Ed said you'd fill us in." He had a voice like a dog chewing on bones. Nice and menacing.

"O.K. Now all I want you guys to do is stand near me. Anything illegal, I'll do it — though this part, at least, is going to be legal enough. It's later there may be trouble. So don't even say a word. Then, later, if it comes to that, you can truthfully say all you did was join me at my request."

"Some part," Tony said.

"Just look like cops," I told them. Gill said, "I was a highway patrolman in *Hell on the High* — "

"Skip that." He started looking unhappy — these actors are all alike — so I added, "Some other time. We've only got a few minutes. Now, here's the scene."

I filled them in. They weren't too happy about it. Especially when I said, "This guy, remember, is not an actor — unless you'd call him a bad actor. He's a hood. If he pulls his heat, I'll shoot him."

In unison, they gulped. "Heat," Tony said. "That's — that's a gun, isn't it?"

"Yeah."

He gulped again. "I'm usually the guy gets shot," he said. "I never played a cop in my life. It's cops that *shoot* — "

"Look, I asked for two guys who'd do damn near anything for a C note. I'll make it two C's apiece if you go through with it. But if you want to back out do it now, and I'll try to pull this off alone."

The big man said, "You think he'll fall for it?"

"I'm pretty sure he will. All you have to do is glare at him."

"Two hundred bucks?"

"Right." I dug into my wallet, got two hundreds and four fifties and held them before me.

Gill took the two hundreds and said, "I'm in."

The shorter one was slower, but he said, "Hell," and took the fifties.

"Good. I don't really think there'll be trouble. Not here. If there is, duck. If there isn't, just follow my lead." I grinned. "And think of what a dandy story this can be for you to tell at the next party. Especially if — Easy." I broke it off. "Here he comes."

Mooneyes had just come inside. He was extending the ticket in his big hand toward the doorman, kind of bouncing on his heels in joyous anticipation of what lay ahead. He didn't appear to have taken time to scrape off the morning's growth of whiskers, but I could smell either powerful powder or a heady after-shave lotion. The wisps of red hair were brushed straight back.

I started toward him.

He saw me. He stopped bouncing in joyous anticipation. The corners of his fat-lipped mouth stretched out and down. He put his hand under his coat. Near his heart. Yeah, he knew where it was; and I didn't think he was taking his pulse.

The last two steps were the longest, but I took them.

"Joseph Garella," I said firmly, "you are under arrest."

Twenty

Those big pale eyes narrowed as the oily, almost lashless lids dropped down to half cover them like a pair of fat eclipses.

"Yeah?" he said. "The hell. You ain't a cop."

Then he turned his head, looked over my shoulder. I risked a quick peek. It was moving along all right. Gill and Tony were thumping across the lobby carpet stern and unsmiling, their gaze piercing Mooneyes.

That's the nice thing about professional actors. When they get their teeth into a part they often really live it, and these two had decided to bite deeply. But when they stopped directly behind me I wondered if maybe the shorter one, Tony — whom I'd thought the more frightened — hadn't bitten off more than he could chew.

He must have seen a policeman in a movie wearing a Detective Special in a holster hung from the left side of his belt. Anyhow, he had his hand sort of pressing his side there, under his coat, and was leaning forward with an expression indicative of severe pain, and he looked like a man gingerly probing his hernia. Maybe he was about to get shot, but he would remain a ham to the end.

"No," I said to Mooneyes, "I'm not a cop. But, in accordance with Section Eight-three-seven of the California Penal Code, one private person may arrest another, and I quote, 'For a public offense committed or attempted in his presence.' So get that into your skull. Mooneyes — all the way into your skull. You're *legally* under arrest."

The sight of the two men behind me had distracted him, but his thick arm was still across his body, hand out of sight. "For what?" he said.

"Suspicion of assault with a deadly weapon. There'll be more, like conspiracy, accessory before the fact of a felony, but the ADW charge is enough for me to hold you. You could get up to ten in Q for that, Mooneyes."

"ADW? What ADW?"

"Think back to last night, Mooneyes," I said. "When you tried to run me down with your heap. Your car was the deadly weapon, and that was sure as hell ADW."

"You couldn't of seen me."

"Knock it off. How do you think I knew it was you, Mooneyes?"

He considered that, and slowly nodded. "By golly, you got me there." He rolled his owlish eyes to the men behind me, then let his right hand drop to his side. "I thought you was comin' in at me," he said, trying on a grin.

"I almost did." We were over the first hump, and I could feel the sweat creep out of me now, under my collar, along my back. "I'll take that itch you were scratching, Mooneyes."

"Huh?"

"The piece." I reached under his coat, slipped out the automatic. He lifted his hand toward it but didn't grab. I shoved the gun into my hip pocket.

"O.K., let's go."

He licked his lips, looked into the darkened theater, at that right-hand aisle down which lay joy, delight, the front row, and a new movement. Then his beefy shoulders sagged.

"You won't make nothin' stick," he said. But he came along with me.

Out on the sidewalk I steered Mooneyes toward my Cad, then stopped and called over my shoulder to Gill and Tony. "I'll take the suspect in. You two follow us."

I was more than a little damp by now. As a gal I once knew might have put it, I was "perspiring a lot of sweat." The scene in the Swank lobby had been merely the first hurdle to get over, and it was supposed to be the easy part. The rest of this operation was the hinge success swung on — first putting the arm on Mooneyes, then throwing the convincer into him, and after that just carrying him along without giving him time to think. Not even the way Mooneyes thought.

But it often happens that, when I get one of my bright ideas, the deeper I get into it the dimmer it appears to me. And this bright idea was no exception. With Mooneyes sitting alongside me on the front seat of my Cad, I used the radio-phone and placed another call to Ron Smith, the guy I'd called before in the Hall of Justice. Mooneyes appeared to be deep in thought, brows furrowed.

When I got through to Smith I said, "What's with Judge Croffer?"

"Left about five minutes ago. Two-hour break for lunch."

I sighed. "Good."

"Not so good. I didn't know there was going to be so damn many of them. Shell, if I get in trouble — "

I couldn't do any explaining with Mooneyes sitting next to me, so I said, "Can it wait? I'll check in with you after I get there. O.K.?"

"Well . . . O.K."

There were questions I wanted to ask — several of them — but they'd have to be asked later, if at all. I hung up.

And Mooneyes, having gone deep enough in thought to find whatever he'd been after, said, "How come you happen to be waitin' so handy there at the Swank? Huh? Tell me that, Scott."

I glared at him. "We knew you'd show up there sooner or later, Mooneyes," I told him truthfully. "It was just a matter of staking out at the Swank till you strolled into our trap."

He said a favorite hoodlum word, adding, "Boy, am I dumb. Walked right into it."

And for the first time in a while I began thinking this might work. Well, from now on that was *all* I intended to think: that it would work, that it couldn't miss.

I pulled out into the traffic, and my two actors fell in behind us. I drove straight to the Hall of Justice, parked, got out, and opened the right-hand door. Mooneyes said dully, "Here?"

"Here."

"This ain't the jail I go to."

"Of course it's not. What's the matter with you? Come on, hurry it up."

The other car was parked by now, and Gill and Tony were walking toward us. Mooneyes got out of the Cad, eyes eclipsing again. I grabbed one of his elbows and ushered him inside the Hall of Justice, up to Judge Croffer's courtroom.

Ed Howell was standing before the big double doors.

We walked up to him and Mooneyes said suspiciously, "What's that big black nigger doin' here?"

Well, you hear about it, but it doesn't often happen right in your ear. I lifted my right hand and was just reaching for Mooneyes when I felt Ed's fingers close around my wrist.

I looked at him, and he winked. On his face was an expression of almost pure delight, a kind of exhilaration. I didn't get it.

He moved his head slightly, then walked off down the corridor. I had to talk to him for a few seconds anyway, so I said to Mooneyes, "You wait here. I'll see if they're ready for us."

"Ready?" His eyes, none too sparkling to begin with, were getting a kind of glazed look. He was confused. Good. I wanted him confused.

I glanced past him to Gill and Tony half a dozen feet away and said, "Watch him, boys."

Gill shrugged as if to say, "Watch him what?", and Tony raised his arms a little, then let them flop. He was no longer acting like a man about to shoot a hood with his rupture.

"But — " said Mooneyes.

I spun on my heel and walked briskly to Ed. "What got into you?" I asked him softly. "That sonofa — "

"Skip it. He gave me an idea — settled a problem for me, Shell." He grinned, then went on rapidly, whispering, "But forget that. I got thirty-six just to sit, best I could do so soon. Four or five people were still here; they didn't leave for lunch. Still *are* here — I couldn't ask them to leave. You didn't say anything about a jury, so I just scattered them around. If you want — "

"That's O.K. Fine, Ed. We'll let the judge try the case."

"Got a great judge. Morrison Blaine, eighty years old and tougher'n hickory. He just finished playing a judge in *The Trials of Elizabeth Dugan*, so he stopped by Wardrobe and picked up his robe and stuff."

Ed's grin flashed in his black face, almost lighting up the corridor. But I was thinking, "robe and stuff"? Robe, O.K.; but what was this "and stuff"? There wasn't time, however, to probe that little detail.

I said, "What about Ron Smith? He was a court reporter once, but when I phoned him he wasn't sure — "

"It's O.K. I talked to him just a minute ago, and he said he'd do it. Not too happy about it, but he's game."

Well, there was plenty more I wanted to know, but there wasn't time. The key to this whole caper was to get Mooneyes off balance and keep him that way. We had to ease him into a strange new world just familiar enough to *seem* real, then start him spinning and keep him spinning — and time or, more accurately, timing, was of the essence.

So I settled for one more question. "You got somebody for prosecutor?"

He grinned again. "Yeah. The district attorney. Me."

I started to tell him the guys with speaking parts were the ones most likely to get into trouble. But instead I said, "Well, maybe it won't come to that, Ed. Let's go."

He opened the double doors. I marched back to Mooneyes and grabbed his elbow again, pulled him toward the entrance. He came along, sort of shuffling his feet. Gill and Tony followed, also sort of shuffling their feet. Tony did that bit with his arms again, up and flop.

The prisoner and I entered the courtroom.

Ed marched ahead of us down the aisle between the rows of seats on our left and right, through the swinging door, and right to a long table before the spectators' seats. A quick glance showed me a nice crowd, and I recognized several familiar faces — a couple of Slade's monsters whom I'd seen outside of their oyster shells, Vivyan Virgin, another young gal I'd last seen wearing something like a gauze bikini and an elaborately jeweled headdress. But now they looked like a gang of citizens gathered to view a trial in Superior Court. Which, of course, is what they were supposed to look like. Up front I saw Ron Smith seated at a little table on which was a stenotype machine. He looked pretty sick, but he was there.

We got almost to the front of the courtroom before Mooneyes snapped out of his daze. I felt a tug on my hand as he stopped, yanking his elbow back.

"Hey," he said. "What the hell? This here is a *court*room."

"Of course it's a courtroom. What did you expect?"

"But I — don't I got to be busted, and my prints took, and arranged first?"

"Arraigned?"

"That's it. Arranged."

I shook my bead. "Mooneyes, don't tell me my job, O.K.?"

"But — "

"An arraignment is bringing the prisoner before the bar of a court to answer an indictment. Right?"

"Uh — "

"Well, that's what we're doing. We're bringing you before the bar of a court."

"But — I got to go to jail first, don't I?"

"Are you an idiot or something? Do you *want* to go to jail?"

"Well . . . Who wants to go to jail?"

"Now you're talking."

While the wheels were still turning in his head, I moved him through the swinging door and left to another long table, got him seated behind it, and sat down next to him.

Mooneyes turned slowly in his chair and looked at the people behind him, looked all around, even at the ceiling. Yes, he was in a courtroom, all right. Couldn't deny that. But something was amiss.

I leaned close to him and said, "Mooneyes, you've got one chance. Turn State's evidence and I'll let you cop a plea. I hear this judge is a tough baby, a regular hanging judge — "

"Hanging? They don't — "

"And if he gets a chance he'll throw the book at you. But if you come clean — about last night, about how Al Gant's been milking the suckers with that sweet blackmail setup, the rest of it — you might get off easy. So be smart, Mooneyes."

He scowled. "You think I'm gonna puke on Al, you're stirry." He looked around again. "I want a mouthpiece. I got a right to a mouthpiece."

There hadn't been enough build-up. I'd gotten him close to the edge, but not over it.

Well, there was no help for it now.

We were going to have to go ahead with it. We were going to have to try him. And sentence him. And maybe even execute him.

I looked at Ed, and nodded.

Twenty-One

Ed flashed some kind of signal to a short thin man sitting near the judge's bench.

He stood up and cried, in a remarkably loud voice for so small a man, "Oyez, oyez, oyez, know all men by these presents that this here court — " He flipped his hand over his mouth while mumbling something unintelligible — "Superior Court, County of Los Angeles, State of California, in these United States, Judge Blaine presiding, is now in session. All of you, rise up!"

I closed my eyes, groaning inwardly. Maybe Tony should have been the tip-off. I had a whole courtroom full of hams. I could imagine what this trial was going to be like: the fragmentary memories of a hundred Hollywood courtroom scenes, half sheer bluff and bluster and the rest, chaos. People might leap from their seats in the audience, fighting to take the witness stand. I felt as if I were coming down with something. Like the hives and heebie-jeebies. And creeping over me was a feeling. A feeling that I was in trouble.

But I'd asked for it. I had to go through with it now. When I opened my eyes the door to the judge's chambers had opened, and striding through it was Morrison Blaine, eighty years old, doddering, smacking his gums, wearing a long black robe and a powdered wig. What in hell, I thought — and where — had those *Trials of Elizabeth Dugan* been conducted? But it didn't bother me. I wasn't going to *let* it bother me. I *wasn't*.

Mooneyes said, "Jumping Jehosaphats. What in hell is *that?*"

"Didn't you hear the guy yelling his name? That's Judge Blaine. The *Hanging* Judge," I added maliciously.

"He looks mean as hell."

"He *is* mean as hell. Well, you had your chance."

"Where's my mouthpiece? Don't I get a mouthpiece?"

"You got one."

"Where?"

"Here."

He looked all around. "Where?"

"Here." I pointed at me.

"*You?*" His eyes were like saucers of milk.

"Me. I'm your mouthpiece."

"Omigawd. It can't be. How can it be? I never heard — Ah, come on. You ain't my mouthpiece."

"You see another one anyplace around here?"

He surveyed the courtroom again. "Damned if I do. But . . . you'll stab me, you'll shoot me down, you'll ruin me, you'll — "

"You bet I will."

His mouth was quite a ways open, and he was breathing through it. Then he clicked it shut. "Somethin' weird is goin' on — "

Bang! The judge used his gavel. "Silence in the courtroom!" Judging by the judge's appearance, I had expected a high, quavering voice to come from him, but the voice at least was O.K. A little cracked, but fairly deep, and strong enough.

"Case of the People versus Joseph Garella . . .," he went on, reading from a slip of paper — which, I assumed, was the basic info Ed Howell must have hurriedly jotted down for him. Too hurriedly. ". . . Known to all and sundry as Mooneyes Garella. Charged with . . . mmm . . . Assault with a DW."

Judge Blaine looked over the, courtroom as if about to launch into a lengthy speech about Justice, Truth, Crime, and Motherhood. It occurred to me that, without a script, it might be difficult to turn these people off.

But Blaine caught himself in time and said, "Take the witness."

Then he looked at the empty witness stand. He looked at it for a long, long time, then sort of shook himself and peered out over the courtroom. His peer came to rest on me, and he smiled in satisfaction. Here was his cue. "Is the witness — mmm . . . defendant represented by counsel?"

I glanced at Mooneyes. His mouth was hanging open again. His eyes were wide. His lower lip was quivering just a trifle. I decided he was ripe; if he'd gone along with this much, he'd go along with anything.

I rose to my feet. "Yes, Your Honor. I represent the victim."

"He *don't!*" That was Mooneyes.

Bang! That was the judge. "Contempt of court. Fifty dollars."

I looked at Mooneyes. "I told you he was mean. Now you've antagonized him."

"Oh . . .," he said. "Uh . . ."

"And the trial hasn't even started yet."

"Fine," the judge said, "fine and dandy. Now, is the pros-ecourter in the cute? Mmm . . . cutor in the court?"

Ed Howell got slowly to his feet. "I'se gwine persecute him," he said.

At first it shocked me — he was laying on that too-long-laid-on Hollywood stereotype of the Negro, the phony burlesque of rolling eyes and the Stepin-Fetchit whining drawl, never seen or heard in the flesh anywhere on earth except a Hollywood sound stage. It shocked me — and others here, too. I heard a few soft gasps, the sudden intake of breath — from some who knew him, some who had worked with him.

But it shocked me only for a moment. Because as Ed continued the thing took on a kind of rhythm; it was starting to play, to swing. And I thought I was beginning to understand the reason for that exhilarated expression on Ed's face out there in the corridor.

More, another look at Mooneyes' face convinced me Ed had hit the right note, twanged the right chord. Because Mooneyes' mouth was open now to its maximum aperture, and it stayed open while he swallowed about once a second, his Adam's apple bouncing.

"*I'se* gwine persecute him," Ed went on, "for assault with a DW and auto battery, for committin' mayhem and raisin' Cain, for ADW and KKK and shootin' people dead!"

One small sound I heard came from Mooneyes' open mouth.

But there were more. A couple of people in the audience said softly, "Yeah!" And I heard the single clap of one pair of hands. There *was* a kind of rhythm and swing and bounce to Ed's delivery that almost made you want to snap your fingers and call out or join in. Those first soft cries had come from two Negroes sitting together on the right side of the courtroom — but immediately after that half a dozen more spectators caught the mood, raised their heads and sighed "Yeah!", and then clapped their hands together. One of them, I was pleased to see, was Vivyan. It takes some of us white folks a little longer to catch the rhythm, but most of us get it in time.

Ed had been standing quite still during his opening remarks, but now he walked around the table, shuffling his feet, while his shoulders sort of hunched forward and then swung back, saying, "Now, he's guilty, ain't no doubt 'bout that." He stopped shuffling and looked at the spectators, leaned forward, and said slowly, "Is they? *Is* they any doubt?"

Well, it wouldn't have come off if Ed hadn't been performing before people he knew — all of them actors, at that. But he'd gotten the message to them, the rapport was near perfect, and it came off.

It was only a little ragged, all thirty-odd simultaneously crying "*No!*", with a few trickling on alone, "They ain't *no* doubt."

All — except five.

Ed had told me "four or five" people had been left over from Judge Croffer's earlier session here in this same courtroom. The number was five exactly. Because five faces looked — well, you can imagine.

Ed was shuffling and slinking again, grinning — obviously enjoying himself. I decided he was a bigger ham than most of the rest put together. He was looking at Mooneyes, moving closer.

I felt a tugging at my sleeve. It was Mooneyes tagging.

"Say something," he said. "*Do* something."

"It's not my turn yet."

"When — when is it?"

"I may not get a turn. It depends."

He didn't like that. "On what?"

"On the judge. And you *already* got him mad at you."

Ed said, "Well, I done proved he's guilty. Now, whatever happens to him is up to the court. I don't care, what it is just so it's plenty. Whatever it is, I agrees with it, just so it's the fullest penalty the laws allows."

Tugging at my sleeve again. Mooneyes hissed, "What's he *mean*, he's proved it? He ain't proved nothin'. He ain't presented no evidence."

I shook my head, looking grim. "That's for the judge to decide," I said.

Ed had turned to face the judge following his last remarks. "Your Honor," he said, "I respectfully suggests two life sentences to run out concurrently, and as soon as possible."

Judge Blaine said, "If I interpret counsel's counsel correctly, you recommend a double death sentence?"

"Perzackly, Judge."

"Sounds reasonable to me," Blaine said, raising his gavel.

"What the hell kind of — " That was Mooneyes.

Bang! "Contempt of court. Hundred dollars."

I looked at Mooneyes, shaking my head. And right then it happened. The farce — if he'd ever really thought of it as one — stopped being a farce. Farce, fraud, frame-up, total madness — no matter; Mooneyes believed it. He was scared.

Put it like this. Did you ever spend a night in jail? If you did, probably at some moment the thought came to you that has come to so many other law-abiding people who stumbled into the can for one night. For a while, after that door clanged shut, maybe it was something to be angry about, or maybe it was almost amusing. But somewhere along in there — inevitably — must have come the realization of your total, your absolute helplessness. You can't get out. There's nothing you can do. Yelling's no good. You can't crash through those walls. *They've* got you, and there isn't a damn thing you can do about it. They can do anything they want to do with you. O.K., so you're innocent. So walk out.

Something like that must have been going through Mooneyes' horrified brainbox. Maybe it was wrong, crazy, impossible — it was happening. *They* had him. If he couldn't get a lawyer — except me — couldn't phone, couldn't get word to Al, couldn't do anything . . . *they* could do whatever they wanted to do.

He tugged at my sleeve again. His usually pink face was pasty. "Scott," he said in a loud, hoarse whisper. He licked his lips. "Scott, I think maybe I'll cop that plea. Yeah, I think maybe I will." He meant it, too.

I turned my head and looked at Ed Howell, near enough to have heard Mooneyes' plea, and I winked.

Then I said to Mooneyes, "I'm afraid it's too late."

Breath sighed out of his lungs like trapped gas from a water faucet. "But . . . but . . .," he said. "You're my *mouth*piece. You *got* to do something."

I said, deliberately, "Mooneyes, I neglected to tell you something. I'm a friend of the DA. I want *him* to win this case."

Mooneyes' eyes got enormous. He looked at Ed Howell. "Him?"

"Him."

Silence. Then he said dully, "Why, you white-haired sonofabitch. You big — "

"That'll get you ten more years."

" — white-haired sonofabitch. You big — "

"Your Honor," Ed said, stifling a grin, "the persecution rests."

"O.K.," the judge said. "Before the court passes sentence on the guilty party, would counsel for the defense care to comment on the comments of the counsel for the offense?"

I stood up.

"Your Honor," I said. "Ladies and gentlemen. Friends, Romans, countrymen."

Ed slapped his thigh. His lips formed the word, *ham*.

I scowled at him and went on, "We have gathered here to bury Mooneyes, not to praise him. As counsel for the condemned crook I must protest that the evidence against my client is so . . ." I paused and glanced at my client. Hope flickered. Flickered and died. "So overwhelming," I continued, "that I have been unable to prepare a proper defense. In fact, I haven't been able to prepare any defense at all. Therefore I would like to request — " I cut it off.

This guy just might misunderstand if I didn't kind of help him to a decision. "Well," I said, "you wouldn't consent to a postponement? You *wouldn't*, would you?"

"Eh? A postponement? What kind of postponement?"

"Oh, say a year or so. It will take that long to — "

Then he got it. *Bang!* "No. Postponement overruled."

"That," I said, "tears it. On behalf of my client, then, we plead guilty and throw ourselves on the mercy of — "

"*No! Not* on a mercy of — " My client wouldn't keep his big mouth shut.

Bang! "Two hundred dollars."

"*No!* You — "

"Five hundred dollars."

"Nnn . . ."

He was really ripe. I leaned over and put my mouth near his ear. "Mooneyes, it looks bad."

"It looks . . ." He'd been in some kind of trauma. Slowly he came back a little. "Horrible."

"You got that part about two death sentences to be executed concurrently, didn't you?"

"Yeah. What's it mean?"

"Means you get executed twice, just to be sure you're dead. First the gas chamber, then electrocution — that's the current in concurrently. You're the con, and — never mind."

"I get it. Means they gonna kill me."

"Yep. You got it."

"I confess. I trow myself on a mercy of the court."

"That's the only chance you've got, Mooneyes. If you'll take the stand, and spill your guts — "

"I'll spill 'em."

"Pour out everything you know about Pike, Waverly, Natasha Antoinette, the works . . ."

He was nodding.

"O.K. I'll see what I can do."

I stood up again. "Your Honor, may I approach the bench?"

"I don't see why not."

"Thank you, Your Honor." I walked up before him, looking into my wallet. There was one lone hundred-dollar bill left, and I got it out, handed it up to him. "Beautiful job," I whispered. "Just right."

He beamed.

"I'm going to put this creep on the stand," I said. "So don't sentence him to torture or anything unless I give you the high sign. But if he slows down, it wouldn't hurt to stick him a little."

Blaine nodded. "I was good, eh?"

"Fine. Keep it up."

I went back to Mooneyes. "You can testify — that is, spill your guts," I said. "It may help and it may not. That's up to you."

He swallowed. "What'd you do up there? I seen you give him something."

"It was a C note. I bribed the judge."

"Smart thinkin' . . ." Hope flickered, and died. "With a C note?"

"That was merely so you could testify. Now get up there, Mooneyes — and sing. O.K.?"

"You bet." He nodded, thinking. "Gonna kill me twice, how about that? Boy, once is plenty. In fack, it's once too much."

"Then take the stand and I'll cross-examine you."

He got to his feet.

I said, "But no games, Mooneyes. Once you start, you'll have to go through with it, the truth, the whole truth, and nothing but the truth."

"Yeah. O.K."

Just to be sure, I added, "You'll have to puke on Al."

He looked at me. "I'll puke all over him," he said.

Then he walked toward the witness stand.

Twenty-Two

"Mooneyes," I said, "do you swear to tell the truth, the whole truth, and nothing but the truth?"

"I hope to shout."

He was seated in the witness stand, and I stood next to him. Beyond him on my right was Judge Blaine, and on my left the spectators in the courtroom.

"That's the spirit," I said. "Where were you on the night of — two nights ago, shortly after nine P.M., when you were driving a black Imperial sedan to Finley Pike's home?"

"That's where I was."

"Where?"

"Where you said. Toolin' the heap to Finley's."

"You and who else?"

"Me at the wheel and J. B. next to me, Hoot and Tom-Tom in back."

"That's J. B. Kester, and Hoot who and Tom-Tom what?"

"If you say so."

"I mean, what are the last names of Tom-Tom and Hoot?"

"Damned if I know. Just Tom-Tom and Hoot. Like, 'Hey Hoot — '"

"Skip it. Why were you racing to Finley Pike's residence?"

"It wasn't no race. We was the only — "

"Why were you in such a sweat to get there?"

"Al told us to do it."

"By 'Al' you mean Aldo Gianetti, commonly known as Al Gant, your — your employer."

"That's him."

"Now, what is — was — the relationship between Al Gant and Finley Pike?"

"They ain't related."

"Strike that. Al and Finley were acquainted, they knew each other, and were — in a sense — in business together. Right?"

"Right."

"What was the business?"

"Blackmail."

Because I was concentrating on the dialogue with Mooneyes, I had almost forgotten the spectators in the courtroom — and the fact that at least thirty-eight of them, counting Ed Howell and Morrison Blaine, were active members of the movie and TV industries and thus individuals very familiar with *Inside*, and with Finley Pike. At least since Pike's death and the revelation that he'd been Amanda Dubonnet.

There was a gasp from those people, a *big* gasp, so big it must have come from nearly all of those thirty-eight throats. The knowledge of blackmail had been so much a part of my thoughts for this past day I'd forgotten that these others knew nothing at all about the Amanda-Pike blackmail operation. That hadn't hit the newspapers yet.

I went on — noting that Ron Smith's fingers were expertly tapping the stenotype keys, "Just tell us, in your own words, about this blackmail business, how it was conducted, and the relationship — association of Al Gant and Finley Pike."

"Back from the beginnin'?" he asked.

"All the way back."

"Well, Al knew Finley quite a spell, four, five years. Put him into some good things from time to time, thinkin' he could get the favors back later. Like he usually done. Couple years ago Al got a bug to start a magazine or a newspaper, so he put up a pile of cash to start one."

"That was the trade paper now called *Inside*?"

"Yeah."

"Did Al choose Gordon Waverly as the man to publish the paper?"

"I wouldn't know about that."

True, there were a lot of things Mooneyes wouldn't know about; but I was delighted he knew as much as he did. I said, "Did Al give the money to Waverly?"

"Beats me. Way I got it, he give the cash to a old beat-up bag name of Willow. He had some kind of dirt on her, so she'd do what he asked her to. She's the one he told to make sure Finley got a job on the paper."

"So Al Gant insisted Finley Pike be employed on the staff of *Inside*, and utilized the services of Miss Madelyn Willow to ensure that result?"

He blinked the big pale eyes, then said, "I guess so. Yeah, that must be what he done. She was to sell him to this Waverly guy."

"Did Al also insist Pike was to write the column, 'Lifelines for the Lifelorn'?"

"Well, that came later. Al had it all planned that way from the start, but he let Pike bring it up hisself after he'd worked on the paper a while. That was the whole idea — get him on the paper and then start him doin' the column."

"Why was it important that he do the column?"

"Hell, that was the whole bit. See, Al wanted his guy on the paper in the first place because, like he said, there was so much dirt in Hollywood you could scoop it up with a shovel. The paper was, like, his shovel — all kinds of dope would come in to a thing like that. About actors, actresses, stars, movie guys — rich people. Then besides — and he figured this'd be the best angle of the whole deal — there'd be all kinds of cats and dolls in trouble writin' to that there 'Lifelorn' column. Some of 'em would be in big trouble, so big Al could bleed 'em good."

There had been a few more gasps and exclamations from the people gathered in court, but all of them were listening silently now.

"Did it work out like that?" I asked. "Did Al Gant in fact — by selecting damaging information from the material gathered by the *Inside* staff, plus that in letters written to the so-called Amanda Dubonnet's 'Lifelines for the Lifelorn' column — come into possession of information about many individuals in and near Hollywood, which he was then able to use for blackmailing those individuals?"

"Say that again."

I repeated the question, breaking it up into three or four shorter chunks, and Mooneyes said, "You know it. Man, even Al was surprised he got so much dirt. Some of it was just from runnin' down leads from the stuff what come into the paper. But the real good stuff was from the letters to Finley."

"You mean the letters addressed to Amanda Dubonnet, the pseudo — the pen name Finley Pike used."

"That's it. Him as Amanda. Some of them letter-writers, you'd think they was *askin'* to have the bite put on 'em. Letters from guys who'd stole from the boss, embezzling, wives and husbands all screwed up with other people's wives and husbands — even a couple of husbands with husbands. Like that actor who starred in — "

"Whoops," I said. "We won't mention the names of people who were being blackmailed. Wouldn't want to get sued. After all, we're not in a court of — whoops. Ah," I paused. "Isn't it true that much of the information valuable to Al Gant in his blackmail operation came from the letters to Amanda, but indirectly? That is, the information was not damaging so much to the person who wrote the letters but to other individuals named or implicated *in* the letters?"

"Oh, yeah. Sure. There was plenty of that. Like some babe would write saying a guy had raped hell out of her, and she'd name who the guy was that raped hell out of her. Then Al would get his hooks into the guy, see? Not the babe that got the hell — "

"I see."

"It was about half and half. Of the ones Al could use, that is. Half was the one who wrote the letter, the other half somebody else named in it. Sometimes they wasn't named, but from what was said Al could figure it out, or run down who was meant."

I turned and walked toward the spectators, back toward the witness stand again, pacing back and forth as I talked. "Your testimony, then, is this. The letters to Amanda Dubonnet were, for the most part, from people in trouble. Sick, confused, tortured people. Some of them people who had committed crimes or transgressions against either legal or moral law and were disturbed, even anguished, by conscience, guilt, remorse, many of them either physically ill or mentally disturbed. They wrote — and that they acted foolishly in doing so isn't important here — for help, or to unburden themselves of some of the weight of that guilt, or for advice. Yet Al Gant, and you and the rest of Gant's men, didn't give a damn about that, did you? You just went ahead and got your hooks into them and bled them white."

He blinked. "What else?" After a short silence he added, "Hell, that's what blackmail is, ain't it?"

Yep, I thought. That's what blackmail is.

Really puzzled, Mooneyes mumbled, "It made 'em easy pickin's."

Still pacing, I said, "Let's take an example of Al Gant's operation. Perhaps this will make the technique clearer — for the court." I glanced at the judge. He was all ears now, too.

"One of the persons who wrote a letter to Amanda," I went on, "was a girl named — well, we'll skip the names. She had gone, again for help, to a psychoanalyst."

I was walking toward the spectators' seats in the courtroom and I saw Vivyan Virgin sit up a little straighter. "An extremely successful Beverly Hills analyst," I continued. "During analytic treatment the phenomenon known as transference is not unusual, which is to say the patient becomes dependent upon or even greatly attached to, sometimes falls in love with, the analyst. The result in this particular case *was* unusual. The girl became pregnant; the analyst gave her a thousand dollars to pay for an abortion, which she did not have; instead, she had the child — but did not tell the father, the analyst. She did, unfortunately, tell Finley Pike. That is, she wrote a — an anguished letter to Amanda Dubonnet."

I saw Vivyan's mouth open and then close in a silent "Oh."

I walked back and leaned on the edge of the witness stand, saying, "The girl wasn't important to Al Gant — but the analyst was. And how he was. Because among his patients were many very wealthy and important figures prominent on the Hollywood scene."

I heard another gasp. It wouldn't have been Vivyan, but I didn't look around to see who it had been. "So, when Al Gant, with his hooks deep in another victim, began blackmailing the analyst, it was — predictably — not merely for money but for the on-the-couch outpourings of each and every one of the analyst's patients. Complete with records, notes, tape recordings . . . A blackmail bonanza — as the result of just one hastily scrawled letter from a single girl in trouble. Who wrote to Amanda. To Finley Pike. To, that is, Aldo Gianetti."

I paused, letting that sink in, then said to Mooneyes, "Isn't that right?"

"Beats me," he said. "I never seen all the letters and stuff, I just know about the general operation. But Al did have a couple psycho — head-shrinkers on the string, I know that."

"All right. Back to the scene at Finley Pike's two nights ago, Mooneyes. How come Al Gant sent you and the others to Pike's?"

"Just before then he got a call on the phone from Finley — Al was in the Apache, you know?"

"You refer to the restaurant Gant owns — through a front, as usual — on Hollywood Boulevard."

"Yeah. Finley told him — I didn't hear him do it, you understand. This is what I got from Al and the boys — what you call hearsay?"

"Sure. Go ahead. That's all right."

"Finley says someone was there beating me — beating the hell out of him. Like to of killed him. Finley told the guy where the file was at."

"The file? Would this be what we might refer to as the Amanda file? The letters to Amanda, which Gant was using for blackmail?"

"That's it. They was in a box, or actually a kind of suitcase."

"Attaché case?"

"I guess. What the hell. But that's what it was Finley was mentioning about. Incidental, Al didn't do the work himself, that was Finley's job. Him, and a associate what did the actual picking up of the cash and payments."

"Uh-huh. The Collector, an unwashed slob with big feet."

"Big? You know it. Hey, how did you know it?" He half-eclipsed his pale eyes again, then said, "Yeah, we figured you must've pooped him. Is that what — "

"Go on, Mooneyes. Finley phoned Gant. . . ."

"Well, Finley told Al he'd spilled to this guy knocking him around where the file was. And the guy was out in the garage looking for it — that's where Finley kept it hid."

"How come Pike was able to make the call? Seems odd the other man would leave him near a phone."

"Finley said the guy must've thought he was out of consciousness. He played — like a possum, see? Anyways, he was able to pull the phone off of the table and call Al. He asked Al to get some of us over there fast before the guy got away with the letters and stuff."

"Who was the guy? The man beating Pike?"

"You got me. Finley maybe would have got to more of that part but they was just a big clunk then."

"Clunk?"

"Yeah. Al says that must've been when Finley got clunked on the head. Al could hear over the phone somebody moving around, or noises anyways, but he couldn't wait and listen. The guy might get away with the file. So Al hung up and raced around getting us boys. Me and J. B. and Tom-Tom and Hoot, we went there — you know, you seen us."

"Yeah. Did the guy get away with the file?"

"Yeah." Mooneyes nodded. "Boy, was Al in a sweat."

"Where's the file now?"

"I ain't exackly sure. But I know Al ain't worried about it no more. He's either got it or he knows where it is."

"Come again?"

"Later that night Al got another call from somebody. And it was about the letters and all. I don't know what else, but it relieved Al. . . . Hey, you was there, Scott. Remember? When he got the call."

"You mean in the Apache? When I walked in on you and Al a little while after Pike was murdered?"

"Sure. You remember."

I did remember. I remembered, too, that Al Gant had indeed seemed relieved following that call.

"Who was on the phone then? Who called Gant?"

"You got me, Scott." Mooneyes was right at home now, leaning back, one leg crossed over the other and swinging slightly.

"That call couldn't have been from J. B. Kester, could it?"

"I don't see how. Al sent him to the garage to see if maybe the stuff was still there. That was before Al got the call. But you know what happened to J. B."

"Yeah. He tried to shoot it out with the police and got killed for his stupidity. O.K., Mooneyes, here's a kind of important question. Why did Al Gant bring in a hood to kill Natasha Antoinette?"

"All I know is he sent outa town for Pete Dillerson, and Pete done it the next morning. Why, I don't know."

"Pete Dillerson is the man you drove to my apartment last night?"

"Yeah. He was watching for the Dayne dame, but a bell-monkey drove her heap up front. So we followed her. When we seen where she drove, Pete says he could kill two birds with one stone." He paused. "Which he was kind of wrong about."

"Except for the fact that Gordon Waverly is publisher of *Inside*, is there any other relationship between him and Al Gant? Are they partners in anything else?"

"I don't know nothing else about him."

"Did you ever see them together? Know of any personal contact between them?"

"None I know of. Could be. Like I said, I just get a thing or two here and there. From Al, or the guys, maybe drivin' the heap someplace. I don't know half of what Al's up to, and that's the truth."

"How about Jeremy Slade? He in anything with Al?"

"Couldn't prove it by me."

"You ever see them together, know of any contacts, meetings?"

"News to me. Did they?"

"I don't know. I'm asking you, Mooneyes."

He shrugged. Then he blinked and said, "Yeah, they's one thing. Just a loan, though. Al loans money out all over the place. Lots of legit guys, when they can't get a loan from a bank, they don't mind gettin' it from Al. He's got so much dough — "

"A loan? To Slade?"

"That's it. I nearly forgot it. He got hard up when he was makin' a picture. Year ago, maybe — no, less than that."

"When Slade was filming *Ghost of the Creeping Goo?*"

"No kidding? That what it was called?"

I scowled at him. "That would have been nine months ago, approximately."

"Sure, about then. He couldn't glom onto the clams anywheres else, so Al give him a hundred-sixty G's."

"Let's get this straight. Jeremy Slade was unable to borrow the money he needed from his bank, so he approached Al Gant — and Gant loaned him a hundred and sixty thousand dollars?"

"That's what I just told you."

"I assume Slade's been paying the money back, or sticking very close to whatever arrangement he made with Gant."

"Ho-ho," Mooneyes laughed softly. "You know it."

I did know it. You either paid Al Gant, and on time, and with a big happy smile, or Al Gant killed you. I said, "Then Slade paid his installments directly to Al?"

"Well, not direct. There might've been talk if he was seen around with Al, you know. So Al fixed it so Slade give the money to Finley. It was O.K. that way, on account of Finley was always around with the movie guys, being a writer on that movie paper."

I guess I'd become a little too interested in Mooneyes' tale myself. And, certainly, I had failed to keep an eagle eye on the passage of time.

I had known Judge Croffer would be coming back from lunch eventually. At least, I should have known. Also, undoubtedly, spectators returning to pick up the thread of that pre-lunch trial were returning, or about to return; but we had the big double doors locked. We didn't have the other door locked, though, the one leading from the corridor into Judge Croffer's chambers.

That became apparent when I looked past Mooneyes and the judge's bench to the far end of the wall, and the door there that led to Judge Croffer's chambers, and became aware that the door was open.

More important, Judge Croffer's head was poked out past it.

He was a large man, with a lot of white hair, rimless glasses, a sharp nose, and small eyes. I didn't know how long he'd been standing there, listening; it couldn't have been long, because he was still standing there. But, slowly, his expression was changing.

It wasn't at all like Jeremy Slade's facial performance. Not nearly so dramatic. This was more subtle. Just a twitch here, the lifting of a lip there, the elevation of an eyebrow. Then his small eyes got even smaller. He squeezed them tightly shut.

Then he opened his eyes, took off his glasses, and looked at them. Why he looked at his glasses I don't know. But that's what he did.

"Court's adjourned!" I yelled.

Bang! "Case dismissed!" Judge Morrison Blaine was already off the bench when I saw him, going at a rapid dodder toward the double doors. They were a long way off. I didn't think he was going to make it.

People were popping up all over the place. There were squeals from a few gals in the audience. Two men were at the double doors. Yelps and exclamations erupted.

Judge Croffer took two quick steps into the courtroom — his courtroom. He stood with his feet apart and hands on his hips and he roared in a voice like thunder rolling down from Olympus:

"Silence! I will have *silence* in this courtroom!"

He got it.

There's something about a *real* judge. . . .

Twenty-Three

I had a hunch this was going to cost me some money.
I had a hunch it might cost me a few years of my life.
I had a lot of hunches. I didn't like any of them.

But — and this was the important thing — no matter what happened to me it would be worth it. A new approach to an old problem, that of softening up a hardboiled hood, had worked out better than even *I* had hoped it would. Of course, I could thank Ed Howell for a lot of it — Ed, and the rest of the people here. All of whom were, perhaps, not exactly happy about being here at the moment.

And that — in this second of frozen silence following the Olympian thunder — reminded me that the whole kit and caboodle was my responsibility. It wasn't just a matter of what happened to me now, but of what might happen to them. This was no time to panic.

So, very calmly, I started walking toward Judge Croffer, then stopped and turned around, and then turned around again, and said, "Bailiff, officers, everybody — watch that man, the convicted . . . the defendant. Don't let him — keep your eyes . . . The hell with it."

Pull yourself together, Scott, I told myself.
Seize the bull by the horns.
Hell, you can *talk* to him, can't you?

I cased the courtroom, got squared away, found a landmark. That was north. There was the judge's bench. Ah, there was Judge Croffer. This time I walked directly to him.

"Judge," I said, "in the memorable words of Mooneyes, I trow myself on a mercy of the court."

Last time, he'd yanked off his glasses and looked at them. This time I got the impression he wanted to pull off his ears. His mouth moving, and his eyes darting about, and his head swiveling on his neck, all at once, presented a picture I would not soon forget.

"I think," he said slowly, "you didn't say what I thought I heard."

"What I mean, Your Honor, I'm guilty, I did it. I accept full responsibility. What I mean, we've just cracked a case here. A big one. That is, if you don't uncrack it — "

"Please be quiet."

I shut up.

He was silent for a moment. Then he asked, "Can you explain this?"

"Yes."

"Are you responsible for the presence of these people in my courtroom?"

"Yes."

"Can you justify this unprecedented breach of propriety, legality, and sanity?"

"Ye — well, I think so. I can come pretty close."

"Who are these people?"

Mooneyes was too far away to overhear us, so I said, "They — they're . . . actors."

"Actors? All of them?"

"Except for the actresses. And one hoodlum. And — "

"Hoodlum? A criminal?"

"And how."

"You're sure of that?"

"Man — Your Honor — I'm positive. We tried him and convicted him — and he confessed to everything but nymphomania."

"Indeed." Silence. "Interesting." Silence. "Who is this hoodlum?"

"Name is Mooneyes. Joe Garella. One of Al Gant's musclemen."

"I am familiar with the records of Mr. Gant and Mr. Garella. And what is your name?"

"Shell Scott. I'm a private — "

"Yes. I am familiar, also, with your record."

He made it sound criminal.

He said, "I think you had better join me in my chambers."

Then he looked past me to the tableau in the courtroom and called, "All of you, return to your seats. Stay in this courtroom. I will speak to you later."

He spoke as if certain that they, each and every one, would do exactly what he said. And I felt pretty sure they would.

Five minutes later I began thinking maybe I wouldn't get ten years. After ten minutes I wondered if maybe I'd get off with six months in the County. But after twenty minutes I was blowing silent kisses to my good fairy.

Judge Croffer turned out to be a very fine fellow indeed. He'd done a few crazy things, too — in his youth, he said. And results — at least, in this case — were what counted. After all, no real harm had been done; the courtroom had been empty; he believed in maximum utilization of public buildings — though not precisely in this manner, no, not precisely.

But if we really did have the goods on Garella, and more important, on Aldo Gianetti . . .

It wasn't quite that simple, of course.

First, when we walked into his chambers, he used his phone to call somebody, and cops appeared from all over the place. Everywhere you looked, cops.

Then he called the chief of police.

Then he called the mayor.

During this time he was getting bits of my story; after talking to the mayor he listened to the rest of it, asked a few questions, then sent for Ron Smith's stenotype record of the "trial." The judge could read the hieroglyphics and ran over the tape rapidly, saying, "Hum," and "Indeed!" and once even "Splendid! Splendid!"

Then he handed the tape back to Smith and said briskly, "Get this typed as rapidly as possible. See Wilkins and have Mr. Garella sign all copies, attesting to its truth and the usual. Get Treacher on the phone and send Borden in here. I'll talk to you later."

Then he turned to me. "You realize this isn't enough that we may legally arrest and hold Mr. Gant, do you not?"

"Yes. But I think there'll be more. I'm not through yet."

"You're not?" He seemed mildly surprised.

"No — that is, I'm not if you don't toss me in jail."

He smiled. "We can, perhaps, avoid that extreme measure." He sighed. "This may be sufficient to assure detention of Mr. Garella. Do you think he will repeat his confession?"

"I think so. He's under arrest, anyway. I arrested him — legally. He tried to commit a felony on me."

"Splendid. Then we needn't worry about that." He paused. "You said you're not through. What did you have in mind?"

I told him. Then he let me call Ed Howell in from the courtroom, and I told Ed. I gave Ed the keys to my Cad and said, "All my machinery and electronic equipment and such is in the trunk. The shotgun mike's the longest thing in there; you can't miss it."

"O.K."

"Be sure Slade's nowhere around when you tip Dale Bannon. He'll go along, won't he?"

"Sure, no worry about that, Shell."

"I'll be out there in an hour. Time enough?"

"More than enough."

I stood up and shook his hand and grinned. "Thanks again, Ed. And — you were great out there, you big black nigger."

He laughed. "You weren't so bad yourself, you white-haired sonofabitch."

He went out.

The judge was frowning. "Did I hear you — "

I interrupted, smiling. "It's a private joke, Your Honor."

Twenty minutes after that I was on my way. To wrap it up — or to get killed. It seemed to me I'd thought that thought before....

I made one stop on the way, to check back copies of the L.A. *Herald-Standard*. From Gordon Waverly's report to me about Natasha's talk with him on Wednesday night, I knew the hit-run accident she'd been involved in had occurred "early this month" of April. I found the story in the *Herald-Standard* for Sunday, April fifth. On the previous night a young man named Theodore Harris had been injured in an accident on Mulholland Drive. He hadn't seen the driver, or the car, which hit him; he hadn't seen anything. He'd just been driving along, then he woke up in the hospital with a broken leg, a fractured pelvis, internal injuries, and a concussion. He was still in the hospital, but recovering.

The information wasn't essential, but I was glad to have it. It helped a little. So, with that final bit of ammunition, I headed for Venus once again.

It was the same old scene, only without the monsters. They weren't working today, of course, and apparently the Venusian queen's head had already been cut off, practically before your eyes.

Cameras and other equipment were being moved several yards to a new location. I saw Dale Bannon, seated behind one of his big cameras, talking to Ed Howell. I gathered this was to be a scene in which

Cherry Dayne had a leading part. Cherry and Gruzakk. Having lopped off the queen's head, presumably he was going to start charming Cherry. Not if I could help it.

I caught Cherry's eye and waved, but there wasn't time for more than that. I spotted Slade talking to Walter Phrye, walked up near the producer, and waited till he looked at me.

Then I crooked a finger at him.

He scowled — and you know how he scowled when he really wanted to — but came over.

"You again," he said in his most menacing tweet. "What in hell are you doing here?"

"I came out to tell you when, and how, and why you murdered Finley Pike."

Twenty-Four

It was a long silence.

He put his upper lip down over his lower lip. Then he put his lower lip up over his upper lip. Then he appeared to be attempting to put them both over his upper lip. He could do more marvelous things with his chops than anybody I'd ever seen before.

Finally he got his mouth untangled and used it to say, "You're a very funny fellow."

"I'm going to get funnier. You want to laugh here? Or do you think maybe we ought to stroll away from the nearby ears?"

He didn't answer the question. Instead he said, "You came out to tell *me* this fairy story?"

"That's right. I'd prefer for you to tell me, of course. Save me a lot of work, and breath. But I guessed it was highly unlikely you'd tell me — unless I told you all about it first. So, that's why I'm here."

He pulled his eyebrow down and rolled his eyes up toward it and then suddenly away, as if he didn't enjoy looking at himself. I guess he was thinking, because then he said, "You're right, Scott, I think we ought to take that stroll."

He led the way. If it had been up to me, I'd have walked just far enough to be sure there was no possibility of our being overheard. But he kept going.

"This is far enough," I said.

He kept going.

It didn't make a lot of difference to me, but I wondered why he wanted to be so far from the other people. I had a hunch it might be important, but there were other things to think about.

When Slade finally stopped, I walked on past, then turned to face him. Beyond him I could see the cast and crew moving around. "Think this is far enough?" I asked him. "You don't want to go on to Nevada, do you?"

"Knock off the chatter. What's this about my killing Pike?"

"Yeah, you killed Finley Pike, all right," I said slowly and distinctly, looking straight at him. "You bashed in his head after coming back from his garage — where you found his file of letters to Amanda Dubonnet — when you caught him making a phone call. You dropped the attaché case and crushed Pike's head with an ivory idol. Right then or very soon after that time, Gordon Waverly arrived and, finding the door open, entered the house — only to be clobbered, also by you. You pounded on Waverly's hands to make it appear he'd been in a fight. Then you put the phone back on the hook and called the police — "

"This is damned silly, Scott I'm supposed to be the guy who did all this?"

"You're the guy. You then left in a great hurry, not only because you called the police but — I'll give odds because you'd heard enough of Pike's conversation with Gant to know some of his hoods would be on their way, too. And if they caught you there they'd kill you. Anyhow, you left in such a hurry you dropped one small piece of paper from the Amanda file across the street. Probably before getting into your car. It was part of a letter from a girl named Jerrilee in which she told of an unfortunate affair with a Dr. Willim Macey."

He reacted at that, but I wasn't quite sure what the reaction meant. He chewed on his upper lip and then seemed trying to take a bite out of the lower one, and he shoved his right hand into his coat pocket. I'd noted a bulge there and for a moment thought maybe he was about to shoot me. But he pulled out a lighter and pack of cigarettes and lit a smoke. It seemed there was still a bulge in that pocket, though, even with the cigarettes and lighter out of it, and I wondered if that was a clue to why he'd wanted us so far away from the other people.

He puffed smoke but didn't speak, so I continued. "Around ten-thirty P.M. you called Al Gant at the Apache and told him you had the file of letters — which to me means that you *had* heard enough of Pike's conversation to know he'd phoned Gant."

Slade had started lifting the cigarette to his mouth, but his arm stopped halfway there. Either he really thought I was out of my mind — that is, if I was wrong about him — or else he'd been stuck by that bit and was wondering where I'd gotten my information. It wasn't quite time to tell him about Mooneyes Garella's singing in court. Not quite.

"Now, about Natasha Antoinette," I said. "You were with her very near the time Pike's collector put the bite on her. And that, or its immediate consequences, not only sent you to see Finley Pike but sent her raging to the *Inside* offices, where she took a shot at Gordon Waverly — a fact which you weren't then aware of. But you both took off in different directions at about the same time, moved by the same stimulus but for different reasons — "

"You're psycho, Scott. Even if any of this made sense, which it doesn't, you'd just be guessing. You can make up any baloney you want about me and Nat, and she can't deny any of it. She's dead."

"Sure. Because you and Al Gant arranged that, too. She can't deny any of it — and she can't corroborate it, either. Which is the reason — or, rather, one reason — she *is* dead. Gant had good reasons of his own, as did you. Besides all the rest, her death also removed the chance your wife would find out about you and Natasha — "

"I'm not going to listen to any more of this, Scott. In the first place, I don't even know this Gant. In the second, there was nothing between me and Nat but just the business relation — "

"Oh, knock it off, Slade." I'd decided it was time to pour it on a little. "We both know you're lying every time you open your mouth."

"You son — "

He'd taken half a step toward me, but I went right on, "Keep your ears open, Slade. Let me lay a few things out for you. One. Nine months ago Vivyan Virgin's absence from the set cost you plenty, when you were on thin financial ice to begin with. Your banker turned down your request for more money — so you went to Al Gant. That sonofabitch gave you a hundred and sixty thousand bucks, which you've been paying back a chunk at a time — through Finley Pike.

"Two. Nat was being blackmailed because she was out with a married man, when the man, drunk, hit another car and left the scene without stopping. Who was the man, Slade? Well, we know she'd been going out with you. And we know that accident occurred twenty days ago, on Saturday, April fourth. But we also know something else: On Saturday, April fourth, *you* had an accident that totally wrecked your Cad but — surprise! — didn't hurt you much. How come? Easy. It wasn't an accident You deliberately wrecked your Cad to hide the evidence that you'd banged into something *before* wrecking it. What you banged into was the rear end of a car driven by a young guy named Theodore Harris, now in the hospital — and SID can prove it, now there's reason to check both those wrecked cars. So, who was the married man with Natasha at the time of the hit-and-run? Who else? He was Jeremy Slade."

His chops were starting to reflect interesting activity, and he opened his mouth to speak but decided not to. I didn't even slow down. "Three. By late Wednesday night Natasha had already told Waverly of writing to Amanda about her troubles. If she kept talking — to me, or the police, say — it would mean big trouble for a lot of people. You see, Slade, blackmail victims are supposed to keep their mouths shut and simply pay. Once they talk they can't be blackmailed. Maybe Natasha had already been hurt too many times, maybe she just didn't give a damn. But obviously she was ready, willing, and able to spill all the beans. And that wouldn't do.

"As far as you were concerned, the whole town, including incidentally your wife and family, would learn of your affair with Natasha, of your cowardly flight after that accident, of the link between you and Pike. And that was the most important thing by then, Slade; by then you'd killed Pike, you were a murderer.

"From Gant's point of view, her story could blow up his lovely 'Lifelines for the Lifelorn' blackmail setup, implicate him, maybe start others of the victims spilling. Maybe you didn't know how much she'd told Waverly, but you and Gant both knew she'd written that letter to Amanda and had built up enough steam to blow the whistle — "

"I never heard so much hot air. Even if any of it was true, it's just guesses — "

"Four. You and Gant agreed Nat had to be killed. Gant brought in an out-of-town hood named Pete Dillerson. The next morning Dillerson shot and killed her. He smoked five cigarettes before he pulled the trigger. Yet she was in plain sight all the time, most of that time sitting in a chair, a perfect target. Still, he waited. Why? Also easy. He waited until the exact moment when she'd finished her *final* important scene in the picture. Your picture, Slade. Who knew when that exact moment would come? Not Pete Dillerson. Not even Gant, unless you told him. The man who knew was you, you sonofabitch."

His features were slack. He realized by now that someone must have talked. So I grinned at him and said, "Sure, Slade. As you've guessed, somebody's been filling my ear with the truth, what really happened. And you're going to the gas chamber. Not only for killing Pike, but for helping to plan Natasha's murder."

I walked past him toward the set, wondering if he'd come along. He didn't. I was about two steps past him — where I wanted to be — when he said, "You're not going anywhere, Scott. If somebody's been filling your ear with what really happened, I guess I'll have to kill your ear."

It was an odd way to put it. But I understood what he meant. Especially when I turned and realized there was no longer a bulge in his coat pocket. The bulge was now in his right hand, and I guessed it was a .32 caliber. Big enough.

"How long have you been carrying that?" I said.

"The last couple days."

"Just since you killed Finley Pike, you mean?"

He said quietly, "That's right. Just since I killed Pike." He paused, then asked me, "How did you know about Pete Dillerson? I didn't even know his name was Dillerson. Only name I heard was Pete."

"Joe Garella — Mooneyes — spilled all he knew and he knew plenty. Put that gun away, Slade. Killing me won't help you."

"It will if you're the only one who knows what you've told me."

"I'm not"

"So you say. But you'd say that to keep me from shooting."

"Believe it or not, I wouldn't. I'm telling you the truth. Maybe nobody else has a hundred per cent of what I do, but better than three dozen people heard Mooneyes spilling. They know enough to cook you, Slade."

"I still think you're lying. I have to think so — what other chance have I got?" His voice was tight, even higher than usual. "I know you carry a gun, Scott." He glanced past me, then at my face again. "When they get out here your gun will be in your hand. I'll say you jumped me, pulled the gun, I was lucky enough to shoot you first." He licked his lips. "If I kill you, I'll get out of this. It'll work."

I knew what was going through his mind. He was convincing himself it *would* work — and at the same time working himself up to the point where he could actually do it. Slamming Pike with a club was one thing. But to stand before a man and look in his eyes and pull a trigger and murder him in cold blood, that is another thing entirely. It would take him a little time to reach that moment of violence — unless I pushed him to it by jumping him. But I wasn't going to jump him. When he reached that moment I had one happy word with which to stop him. Or try to. One word — and I hoped it was the right word.

In the meantime, while he still wasn't ready to pull the trigger, I meant to keep him talking. And this was a time when he would probably talk freely, be glad to talk.

"Listen, Slade," I said quietly. "It won't work. I know you and Gant set up Nat's murder. But I was right about you and Natasha too, wasn't I? The hit-run and the rest of it?"

"Right enough. Nat and I had a big thing going for a couple months. I wanted to drop it; she didn't. The night when I ran into Harris was the last date we had." Sweat glistened on his forehead. "But she kept calling me up. I told you the truth about going to see her Wednesday night. She called me. But it was because she'd just been slapped with the blackmail business — about the hit-run and the rest of it. Well, that was bad enough. Worse was finding out how that baldheaded bastard learned of it, finding out she'd written a damn fool letter to Pike — I mean to Amanda Dubonnet. That told me who the real blackmailer was. I chewed hell out of Nat, slapped her around a little, then took off to see Pike."

"How come you knew he was Amanda? Not many people were in on that."

"I owed Gant plenty and was paying him off through Pike, so I saw him pretty often. One night he let it drop about the Amanda column — just that he wrote it, not the blackmail part. Hell, I didn't know he was using the letters for blackmail until that night, from what Natasha told me, and I didn't realize Gant was behind it himself till I heard Pike talking to him on the phone."

"Uh-huh. Anyway, you went there and banged Pike around. How come your hands weren't marked up?"

"I knew I was going to slug him when I went there. That's *why* I went there. So I wore a pair of driving gloves I had in the car. It was the blood on those gloves gave me the idea to bang Waverly's hands with that idol."

"You didn't go there to kill Pike, then?"

"Hell, no. I went there to get that damn fool letter Nat wrote him. I grabbed the whole case of them when I found it — that was when I heard Pike on the phone. You're right about that, Scott, only I didn't just hear part of the conversation — I heard it all. It was short. I went for him, swung that idol at him, trying to shut him up before he could give Gant my name. I wasn't fast enough."

"You mean he actually told Gant you were the guy who'd pounded on him?"

"He sure did. I remember every word. All he said was, 'Al, this is Finley. Get Mooneyes and the boys over here fast. Slade's just beat the hell out of me. I'm supposed to be out cold and he's in the garage looking for the file.' I hit him then. Not to kill him — just to shut him up. Maybe I'd started for him and couldn't stop; it was fast. Maybe I hoped Gant might not have understood him. Anyway, I slugged him. Then . . . well, when I realized he was dead, then I had to start worrying about Gant."

"Because if Gant knew you were the guy there in the house, he'd soon know you'd killed his boy, right?"

"Sure, just as soon as he found out Pike was dead. I was really in a sweat — and then Waverly drove up, charged up to the door. Hell, I had to knock him out. Talk about sweat — Pike dead, Waverly on the floor, Gant's men on their way to the house."

He stopped, his face stretched into a fascinating contortion. But I looked at him almost in admiration. I finally understood, fully, why he'd called the police then — and I had to hand it to him. I said, "So you called the cops."

"Yeah. Called them, and lit out."

"The cops would probably arrive before Gant's men — which meant Gant's hoods wouldn't even get inside the house, wouldn't know for a while that Pike was dead, wouldn't know the letters were gone — you did take the attaché case, didn't you?"

"I *had* to take it then. The police would probably think Waverly'd killed Pike, and there was a chance Gant would think so, too. He might even think Pike had said Waverly's name on the phone, instead of mine; they sound a little alike. But I had to take the file — couldn't let the cops get it, along with Nat's letter. And Gant would know damn well Waverly couldn't have taken it. Hell, mainly I had to have time to *think*. I knew that bastard Gant would kill me if he even suspected I'd done Pike in or taken the file. But, later, I figured he had two good reasons not to kill me — I owed him money, and I had the letters. I was pretty sure Gant wouldn't touch me as long as I had those letters of his."

"But if you gave them back to him — "

"I'm not that dumb. They're still in a safe place."

"Where?"

He was through talking. "That's all, Scott," he said. "I hate to do this, but — "

But he was going to do it. I saw the sudden tensing of his features, knew he was just about to pull the trigger.

"Smile!" I shouted.

It stopped him just long enough, the unexpected word startling him. "Huh?" he said.

"Smile!" I said again. "You're on *'Candid Camera.'*"

"Huh?" he repeated. Then, silence.

After a few seconds he looked past me to the cast and crew of *Return of the Ghost of the Creeping Goo.*

"Yeah," I said, "you've got it. Dale Bannon is over there with a big camera trained on you, taking your picture. Ed Howell is holding a directional mike aimed at your chops. It was all aimed at me while I told you what you'd done, and it was on you while you admitted it — enough of it. More, to tell the truth, than I expected you to admit."

He swung his head back to me. "Camera?" he said stupidly. "You mean — "

"I mean, this time, you're the star of the picture." I smiled at him. "Which seems appropriate, at last. In all your movies, Slade, you've been the real monster."

I was still smiling at him, but he did not return my smile. As the realization sank in that our actions were being captured on his own film, and that our words — especially his words — were being picked up and recorded, something seemed to snap in him. To snap, and bend, and sway, and crackle, and pop.

I had seen the nearly horrifying metamorphosis of his features once before, in his library-den, but then he'd been *acting*. This was the real thing. This was the unwilling astronaut, not going up slowly, but coming rapidly down. There was a kind of shrieking silence echoing on his chops. His eyes disappeared *completely* as his eyebrow came down like a bat's wing and then wobbled in several directions. His lips peeled up and slid down and sideways. A hoarse grunting sound snuffled from the midst of that tangled mass of tortured physiognomy. He looked — well, I can't describe it because I'd never seen anything quite like it.

But I'll try. You know that stuff Dr. Jekyll drank? And it turned him into Mr. Hyde? Well, Slade looked like what you'd get if Hyde drank it.

I'll admit, I got so fascinated I forgot about the gun in his hand. For perhaps a different reason, he forgot about it, too.

He dropped the gun. I thought maybe he was going to start clawing at his throat, going "Ahcckk, orrckkk," but he didn't. He'd been had, and he knew it. And, finally, he accepted it. With, I thought, a kind of awkward grace, considering the position he was in.

He looked past my shoulder to the movie crew, then at my face, and finally at the people and equipment on location again — as if gazing upon his handiwork for the last time.

Then he lifted his arms and let them flop loosely, much as Tony had done earlier, back in the Hall of Justice.

"Well," he said dully. "I guess my *Goos* are cooked."

Twenty-Five

Much later that same night I was in my apartment at the Spartan. The combination of Mooneyes' courtroom testimony, repeated for the police, plus the "rushes" of the film and tape of my session with Slade, had been, as one policeman put it, "a little bit more than enough," and as a result Slade, plus much of L.A.'s hoodlum population — including Al Gant — were in jail.

After leaving the police I had spent half an hour with my delighted client, Gordon Waverly — who, incidentally, was cheerfully picking up the tab for my courtroom scene — then I'd come home, cleaned up, cooled the gin, and called Cherry Dayne.

Cherry Dayne had said Yes, she'd love to come over for Martinis and charcoal-broiled steaks.

So now life sort of hung, poised, where it had been forty-eight hours before. Only there was a difference. A big difference. Instead of that blonde babe saying, "I'm *hungry*," it was luscious Cherry Dayne seated near me on the chocolate-brown divan saying, "My, that's a *good* Martini."

"Isn't it? The third one is always better."

We'd been talking about the case — part of the time. I'd told her some of the things that had been brought out after Slade's Hyde-de-Hyde performance, most of it at the L.A. Police Building. Now I summed it up for her.

"Slade had been worrying about the hit-and-run accident — and his affair with Nat — even before that big-footed collector put the bite on her Wednesday night. Any kind of leak would ruin him, and he was afraid if he broke off with her she might spill to somebody. Like his wife. Then, when he found out about the letter to Amanda, he quite naturally flipped clear up in the air. Told her to go to hell, they were through, and so on, then raced to Pike's."

I paused, thinking about some of the more significant aspects of the case, then looked at Cherry and said, "Both Nat and Slade were vulnerable to a kind of blackmail — unfortunately — even without the hit-run, you know. Even if he hadn't been married."

"Oh?" Cherry turned the brilliant blue eyes on me, laying on me some of that electricity that makes the world go around.

"Sure," I said. "See, here was this sour, miserable, warped Scotch-English-Norwegian-Irish-Italian-American boy, Jeremy Slade. And here was this sweet *Negro* American girl, Natasha Antoinette. Well, hell, they were going out together. *Together.*"

"How terrible!" she said in mock anguish. "They *deserved* to be blackmailed."

"Of course," I said. "I think Slade even had a little Chinese in him."

She laughed. "Now you're fooling with me."

"Not yet . . . um. Anyway, after leaving Pike's with the Amanda file — which the police have now, by the way — he realized that possession of the letters might convince Gant he should cancel Slade's fat debt. Which Gant did, once Slade got in touch with him and saw him that night. Nat was still a danger to Slade, of course — not to mention Gant — in fact, even more so than before. Well, Gant insisted she had to be killed, and Slade went along with it. So they set it up, and you know the rest."

Cherry asked me, "Slade went back to see Nat later? Is that what you said?"

"Yeah. After getting away from Pike's he called Gant and arranged to meet him later, then went to see Natasha. He made sure she stayed with him — so she wouldn't talk to anybody else. I suppose it's a good thing he did, from his point of view, because otherwise I'd have been able to get in touch with her. But it didn't help him in the long run. I think he might even have killed Natasha himself that night, if he'd had the guts for it — and if he hadn't wanted to be sure she finished her part in his picture first. He was quite a son — quite a fellow."

Maybe Slade hadn't meant to murder Pike, I was thinking; and once it was done I could understand his conking Waverly, who otherwise could have tagged him for the murder; but he had sure as hell known exactly what he was doing when he'd told Gant when his triggerman should knock off Natasha. He swore he was sorry about all of it now, very sorry. Sure he was sorry — he'd been caught.

I finished it up, "Anyhow, Mooneyes realizes they're not going to kill him twice, or even once, but that he'll do another bit in Q. And Gant and a bunch of hoodlums are headed for prison, some of them for the gas chamber." I paused. "That is, unless some kindly old judges decide those bad boys have already suffered enough because of deprivation in childhood, or something. Ah, well, let's not worry about that tonight — at least Slade's kaput, the *Goo* is finally dead, and the world is saved from that."

While we'd been talking Cherry had gotten up and been wandering around the room, looking askance at my big oil painting of nude Amelia, happily at the tropical fish. She was over near the hi-fi set now. Or, rather, the cabinet housing my stereo speakers.

Playing at the moment was De Falla's *Ritual Fire Dance*, and I said, "That reminds me. Why don't I light the charcoal? Then we can dance around it letting out whoops — "

"You're really going to charcoal those big steaks in here?"

"Sure — ah, I went through this once before."

"You did? When? With whom? Did you — "

"It isn't important. But, Cherry, why not? I mean, why not cook them here? It will probably be *loads* of fun."

"But there's no place for the smoke to go, Shell. Like a chimney or anything. Shouldn't — "

"Stop it. I won't listen. I won't have negative thinking. This is my — my big chance. A challenge. My do-it-yourself fire. And there you stand — "

"Oh, go ahead and light it."

I doused the coals with fire juice and lit it. It got going very nicely. This was going to be grand. By the time I'd mixed new Martinis it was just a little smoky in the living room. But just a *little*.

Cherry was still standing by the hi-fi speakers, peering at something. "Oh," she said, "there's a little bug. A spider."

She didn't sound panicky, so I walked over and looked at it. "Yeah," I said. "It's a hi-fi bug." I handed her the new Martini. "I, uh, haven't swept over here for a week."

"Swept? You sweep way up there?"

"I mean mopped, dusted — whatever the hell you do. Actually, I haven't done anything in this whole area for . . . Want me to kill it?"

"Goodness, no. It's sweet."

"It is, huh? Well, in case you were worried, I wasn't going to kill it. I don't go around murdering defenseless — "

"It's a daddy long-legs."

"It sure is, isn't it? Fat one, too."

"Maybe it's going to have babies."

"No kidding. Must be a mama daddy long-legs." I shook my head. "Dear, I'm damned if I brought you up here to look at spiders. In fact, it's the first time anything like this has happened. I *will* kill it. I'll murder — "

"Shell? What's happening?"

"I'm about to kill — "

"No, I mean — look."

She pointed. But I didn't have to look. It was all around me. Between us. Everywhere. Smoke.

"How in hell can that little bitty dib of charcoal put out so much — "

"Shell, it smells like . . . could your carpet be burning?"

"How could my carpet be burning? I didn't light the carpet. Or . . . did I? No, I couldn't have. Hey, I think we better lay off these Martinis."

"Shell, I'd swear your carpet *is* burning."

"Well, the only place it could *possibly* be . . . oh, oh."

I went over to the dandy little Japanese brazier and lifted it up, and looked, and said, "How about that? The damn carpet's burning."

I'd used a lot of that fire juice, I remembered, and possibly a bunch of it had dripped down onto the carpet. Probably. In fact, that's what had happened. I started feeling mean.

"Well, get some water and pour it on it, Shell. Get some *water* — "

"Ahhgg, you sound like — I *will* get some water. Just keep your pa — hold your horses." My eyes were watering. Maybe I could hold my eyes over the carpet and put the fire out. "I'll take care of everything," I said confidently, "just as soon as I find the water faucet. It's in the kitchenette. Wherever that is."

Shell, hurry. *Hurry!*"

"Will you shut . . . I'm hurrying. Here, I'm in the kitchenette. . . . Here's the faucet. Hear the water? I'm getting it now. Just don't *say* anything. There. Here's two glassfuls. . . . Hmm. O.K., I'll get two more glassfuls. . . . There. See, the fire's out. Practically."

"Shell."

"Yeah?"

"It's all right. I wasn't hungry, anyway."

"Well, that's a switch."

"Maybe we can cook the steaks later."

"Yeah. Right now, why don't we go into the bathroom and get a razor blade, and open all our vei — "

"Oh, Shell — that doesn't sound like you!"

"You're seeing the other me. The real me. The mean me. Let's go into the bathroom and fill the tub and — *drown* ourselves."

"Oh, it's not the end of the world. We can air the place out, and in half an hour we'll be laughing about it."

"*You* may be laughing. Ah, it was going to be so grand. It was going to be so — fooey. Well, no sense just standing here strangling. O.K. Let's open the windows. And the front door. And we could at least go into the bedroom and stick our heads out the window, or something, until the smoke clears."

"Do what? Shell, we could go where?"

"Into the bedroom. . . ."

Then I noticed the look on her face. And the smile she was smiling. And in that moment I stopped mentally cursing the smoke and the carpet and the steaks and the fire juice. None of it really mattered. Not when Cherry was smiling the way she was smiling.

It wasn't like that other one, the quavering, down-at-the ends smile. No, this was a real, warm, wonderful smile. But the words were the same:

"Shell," she said, "I thought you'd *never* ask me. . . ."

Biography

Richard S. Prather

Richard Prather is the author of the world famous Shell Scott detective series, which has over 40,000,000 copies in print in the U.S. and many millions more in hundreds of foreign-language editions. In 1986 he was awarded the Private Eye Writers of America's Life Achievement Award for his contributions to the detective genre. He and his wife, Tina, live among the beautiful Red Rocks of Sedona, Arizona. He enjoys organic gardening, gin on the rocks, and golf. He collects books on several different life-enriching subjects and occasionally re-reads his own books with huge enjoyment, especially STRIP FOR MURDER.

LaVergne, TN USA
30 December 2009
168549LV00003B/121/A